Rattlesnake Run

Rattlesnake Run

KEO FELKER LAZARUS

illustrated by Ken Nisson

FOLLETT PUBLISHING COMPANY

CHICAGO  NEW YORK

*To Caroline Gordon, who showed me
how to put the horse before the cart.*

J

L

Library of Congress Catalog Card Number: 68-10480

First Printing
Follett Publishing Company
1010 West Washington Boulevard
Chicago, Illinois 60607

T/L7430

Rattlesnake Run

1

ADAM VANCE pushed the coarse canvas tent flap aside and stepped out into a blaze of blinding light. The summer sun was setting over the low shoulder of hills in the west. Its horizontal rays seemed to pry under his eyelids. Adam raised a sunbrowned hand and shaded his blue eyes. Beneath his bare feet he could still feel the sun's warmth in the yellow caliche clay. Its hard-packed surface stretched in all directions from the small tent to the brush fence close by. This low fence enclosed the compound except for a six-foot opening where his father had pushed the brush aside to back the mail wagon in, that afternoon. The sharp branches of hog plum and mesquite wedged between the cedar palings were all that separated him from the miles of wild Texas brushland beyond.

He could smell the fishy odor of the drying tank a hundred yards to his right. The white lines of earlier water levels ran around this spring-fed pond and across the low limestone ledge on the opposite side. Deep footprints of javelina, armadillo, coyote, and rabbit crisscrossed the sticky yellow mud near shore. Placid now in the still warm air, the water mirrored the bright glare of the sunset. It reminded Adam of the new ten-dollar gold piece his Uncle Seth had given him only last week. It had been Adam's thirteenth birthday.

A mockingbird perched high on a cholla cactus to his left called "Ger-trudy, Ger-trudy, Ger-trudy" over and over. It was the same song the mockers sang back home when they nested in the princess vine on the front gallery. The oblong green pads of a prickly pear cactus studded with dusty purple fruit scalloped the northern skyline. Above him a turkey buzzard, dark wings motionless, spiraled in the warm upward drafts. It banked in widening circles, wobbling slightly from side to side. Adam wondered what scent from below had drawn it here.

Reba, Adam's small black dog, sat down and scratched her left ear, then nuzzled against his knees. Her soft brown eyes looked questioningly up at him. He patted her sleek head. He knew she was wondering why they were here. The two Plymouth Rock hens his father had left that afternoon walked testily toward the brush fence. They eyed the caliche with heads cocked first on one side, then on the other. Adam glanced about. He wondered where he could put the dry-grass nests they would need if they were to furnish eggs. Now squawking querulously, they were trying the mesquite branches for roosting places.

With the light and warmth and sound of day all about him, Adam knew there was little to worry about.

But despite this knowledge, he felt a strange fear creeping into the pit of his stomach. For in this tiny mail station between Rio Verde and Ryansville it would be Adam's first night alone.

He stooped and picked up the dusty bedroll of faded quilts tied with cotton clothesline rope, which his father had thrown down from the mail wagon. The top of the tent was glowing from the last rays of the sun as if a lantern had been hung inside. Adam lifted the tent flap and went in. He dropped the bundle on the hard cot he had just set up against the left wall, and fumbled with the rope knots.

It was hot and stuffy inside. He pushed back his thick dark hair and wiped his sweaty forehead on a wrinkled shirt sleeve. Reba trotted into the tent and sniffed loudly at the sacks of bacon, flour, sugar, and coffee stacked against the right wall. She brushed against the coffeepot. It tipped over onto a cast-iron skillet below. The skillet lid fell off with a clatter. Adam jumped. His startled heart pounded against his ribs. He turned and aimed an angry kick at the dog's smooth black flanks. Immediately he felt remorse. He squatted down, put his arms around Reba's neck, and held her dark head against his face.

"I'm sorry, Reba, I'm sorry!" he said. Reba's warm tongue licked his ear. Adam wondered why was he so jumpy. He could handle this mail station by himself. He had been sure of it when his father had left a few hours ago. Why did he feel this way now? Hadn't his father left him a gun? Adam glanced at the .44 Winchester

9

which stood with his fishing pole in the corner behind the cot. Even though he was small for his age, Adam could handle it. He was a pretty fair shot with rabbits. Adam stroked the dog's glossy back. He was glad he had Reba with him.

The sun was leaving the tent top now, and dusty shadows pushed out from the corners and around the sacks of supplies. Adam sat on the edge of the cot and undid the knots of clothesline rope. He unrolled the bedding, still warm from lying in the sun, and smoothed it down the middle of the cot. He reached into the corner, lifted the Winchester, and laid it on the bed. Carefully, he loaded it with shells from a box on top of the food supplies. Even though he could probably scare any coyotes away by yelling at them, he thought it might be a good idea to have a gun ready.

He left the gun on the cot and stepped outside again. It was still light. A chuck-will's-widow called plaintively from the scrub cedar near the tank. The nighthawks circling high above in the pale sky answered with sharp cries. The evening air felt cool against his face. Adam suddenly realized that he had gathered no firewood, and the night might grow cold.

Picking up an ax that lay with a shovel beside the tent, he ambled toward the opening in the fence. Reba trotted ahead of him. She held her black tail in a graceful curve over her back. The white tip bounced jauntily from side to side. Adam walked too close to the brush at the entrance and caught his shirt sleeve on a sharp twig of hog plum. He stopped to loosen it. Before dark he must not forget to pull this brush back into place, he reminded himself.

A large brown tarantula lifting long silky legs stepped carefully from under a purple sage bush. Adam stopped short, and the spider retreated at the vibration of his step. He glanced down at his bare feet and wished he had brought his boots. There would be scorpions, too . . . he *must* watch his step!

He found the bleached skeleton of a scrub cedar standing worn and twisted near the tank. He lifted his ax and struck the dead trunk a hard blow. There was a dull sound. The cedar tilted over with a slow ripping noise. It reminded Adam of how his last baby tooth had come out of his lower jaw. From the cedar's hollow center poured the black and orange bodies of two six-inch centipedes. Adam jumped back and watched the shiny poisonous creatures ooze like quicksilver to the shelter of a dried grass clump. He jarred the trunk with the ax again and waited cautiously to make sure there were no more centipedes in it. Then he grabbed hold of a crooked root and tugged hard. It was heavy and awkward to drag. The branches caught on the brush fence when he pulled it through the opening. At last he dropped it in the clearing before the tent.

It was growing dark now, and Adam worked quickly to chop the cedar into pieces that would burn easily. The chips fell about his feet. He liked the sharp clean smell that rose from them. It reminded him of the chips from the big cedar by the front gate back home in Ryansville. The wind had blown this tree down last week, and Uncle Seth, who had stopped by on his way home to Rio Verde, had helped Adam chop away the limbs. Uncle Seth had stayed to supper that night, and they had invited Doc Anders, too. It was after supper, when they were all sitting on the front gallery, that Uncle Seth had given Adam the ten-dollar gold piece.

Juanita Lopez, their housekeeper, had baked a big chocolate cake for his birthday. It had been devil's food cake, and his older sister Becky had iced it with thick white frosting. Becky had cut another fat wedge with a candle on it and slipped it onto Adam's plate. It had been his third piece. Adam had eaten until he was so stuffed he could hardly swallow the last dark delicious crumb.

His father had smiled at him with sharp blue eyes. A thick dark mustache covered the corners of his father's mouth, but Adam knew his lips were smiling, too. "That's the way to eat, Son," his father had said and then looked at Doc Anders. "Puny for a thirteen-year-old, wouldn't you say, Doc?"

Doc Anders lifted a pudgy hand and adjusted his gold-rimmed glasses before he peered through them at Adam. "Seein' as how he was the littlest baby I ever delivered in Ryansville, I think he's done just fine."

Uncle Seth, tall and rangy himself, leaned his tan elbows on the table and looked at Adam with his kind brown eyes. "Well now, I wouldn't say he's puny . . . small for his age, maybe, but he'll stretch out directly."

His father, heavy-chested and muscular, squinted affectionately at Adam through half-closed eyes. "Favors

12

his mother, God rest her soul. When I was his age I was twice his size . . . could drive six head of oxen, plow all day with a team of ornery mules, and split a cord of cedar stakes in half an hour."

Juanita, who had just brought the coffee in, put a chubby hand on her ample hip and flashed dark eyes at Joe Vance. "The hummingbird is swifter than the eagle, Señor Vance. I have raised a fine son for you. Do not belittle him."

Joe Vance raised protesting hands. "Don't get your feathers up, Juanita. I only said he's small."

Uncle Seth smiled reassuringly at Adam. "I never was much bigger till I was fourteen . . . sprouted overnight like a ragweed. Give him time, Joe, he'll get there." Adam's thin face and neck had turned a dull red during the discussion.

Joe Vance turned to his brother. "Remember that contract for the U. S. Mail run between Ryansville and Rio Verde we applied for?" he asked.

Uncle Seth nodded. "Cy Connley got it, didn't he?"

Adam's father grinned. "He offered it to me today."

"Sure enough?"

Joe Vance placed his big hands on the table edge. "Says he couldn't keep anyone on the halfway station."

Uncle Seth looked puzzled. "That's funny."

"Says he tried four different men. Every man jack of them left before he got them broke in."

Becky looked up. "Maybe it was Indians scared them away."

Doc Anders laughed. "Honey, I haven't patched

13

up an arrow wound for twenty years! Hasn't been any Indian trouble in this part of Texas since 1875." He turned to Uncle Seth. "That was the date of the last skirmish, wasn't it?"

Uncle Seth nodded. "About then I'd say, give or take a few years." He shook his head. "Nope, wasn't Indians. Appears to me he picked the wrong men . . . shiftless no-accounts, I reckon."

Adam's father stroked the corners of his mustache. "Think we could handle that mail run, Seth? You could drive up from Rio Verde. I'd drive down from here."

Uncle Seth put his hands behind his head. "We might could, but who'd *we* get for the halfway station?"

Doc Anders turned to Joe Vance. "Got a nephew, Frank, comin' out to visit me this summer. Wants to see the West. Maybe he'd be interested."

"It's a thought, Doc, but we'd need someone pronto."

Adam leaned forward. He remembered that station out in the brushland. He had ridden by it with his father only last week when they were quail-shooting. It had looked like a small hunter's camp with a brush fence circling the tent. He had thought at the time how snug it looked in the wild backcountry. Why would anyone want to leave it?

Becky reached across the table with the coffeepot and filled her father's cup. "What would the mail station helper have to do?" she asked.

Joe Vance took a long sip of the steaming coffee. "Not much. Just fix some vittles for Seth and me when we drove in around noon and water the horses while we ate. After we'd hitched up, exchanged mailbags, and headed home, he'd have the rest of the day to himself."

Adam liked to camp. He'd been on several hunting trips with his father. The brushland was full of game. He turned to his father. "How about me, Pa? How about me runnin' the halfway station?"

Tilting his big frame back in his chair, Joe Vance smiled at his son and shook his head. "Afraid you're too young, Son."

"But Pa, I know how to cook. And I can shoot, too!"

"I know, Son, but this is a man's job. Besides, you'd get lonesome out there with no one to play with."

"I wouldn't need to play with anyone. I could take Reba with me. She's fine company and a good huntin' dog, too."

Joe Vance folded his arms across his big chest. "You're just a boy, Adam. You couldn't handle the work it would take to run that station. Nope, sorry. We need a man."

Uncle Seth leaned forward. "Now wait, Joe. Seems to me that Adam here could manage it all right. He knows how to hunt and cook . . . wouldn't need to do much more . . . no schoolin' to fuss with in the summer. Let's give him a try."

"Sure, Pa, let me try. One thing you needn't worry about—I won't up and leave like Cy Connley's men did."

Uncle Seth nodded. "We could depend on you, sure enough."

Joe Vance brought his chair down slowly. "I don't

think a tyke like you could handle all the things that might come up. They tell me the coyotes are gettin' mighty bold out there—drouth drives them mad sometimes. Remember, Adam, it isn't like livin' close to town where you can go runnin' for help when you need it."

"What would I need help for? I'd keep the old Winchester with me." Adam looked earnestly at his father. "*Please* let me go. I could manage the station, I *know* I could!"

Adam's father rubbed his chin. "Tendin' a mail station and campin' for fun aren't quite the same. You're still only a boy . . ."

"I'm thirteen now. I'm not a child anymore."

Becky looked at her father. "You could save some money, Pa, if you let Adam help."

Uncle Seth nodded. "That's right. If we keep it in the family, we might make a little on the contract."

Adam felt sure this would weaken his father's resistance. "You *bet* we could! I wouldn't need much— just a little flour, salt, coffee and a barrel of water. We could take along a couple of hens for eggs, and I could shoot rabbits and quail and maybe a javelina for dinner." Already he could see himself turning a wild pig on a spit over the hot coals.

Joe Vance's eyes twinkled. "You might have to shoot other things too, Son, like pesky coyotes and rattlesnakes."

Adam grinned and tossed the dark hair out of his eyes. "Uncle Seth says coyotes scare easy. I wouldn't have to waste bullets on *them*!"

His uncle pushed back from the table and stood up. "Yep, all you got to do, Adam, is wave your arms in the air like this." Uncle Seth flapped his arms up and down wildly and shouted in a high falsetto, "Git, you yellow cowards, git!" He looked so funny that everyone burst into laughter.

And so, persuaded by his brother and his son, Joe Vance had reluctantly agreed to let Adam tend the mail station.

Adam chopped another branch from the cedar trunk and threw it onto the pile beside the tent. This stay in the mail station should be fun. There really wasn't anything to be afraid of. He was old enough to take care of himself. After the noon meal was over, Adam could do anything he wanted to . . . go hunting, or even fishing in the tank. He paused a moment to watch Reba. She had found a horned toad and was teasing it with nips and barks. The tiny dust-colored animal slithered into the safety of the brush fence.

It was almost dark now. He had thrown the last piece of cedar onto the woodpile when the thin wail of a coyote, eerie and chilling, floated out of the dusk. He had heard coyotes before when he camped with his father. It hadn't bothered him then. Maybe it was the warm light of a campfire he needed. Adam dropped to his knees and scooped a handful of bark and twigs into a small pile between the two metal supports his father had driven into the hard caliche that afternoon. Another coyote howled and barked five shorts barks. The hair on the back of Adam's neck began to prickle. He leaned back on his heels, reached into his pocket, and pulled out a sulphur match. His hands shook as he struck it, and the light went out. Angrily, he threw the match on the ground and reached into his pocket for another. His stomach was knotting up again. Carefully, he held the burning match to the little pile of kindling. A tiny cloud of thick white smoke curled languidly from the smoldering bark. Would it never catch fire? He fanned vigorously with his hand. A leaf glowed red. Then, with a sudden puff, the bark burst into flame.

The howls sounded nearer. Impatiently, Adam fed the fire with more twigs, then large chips and smaller branches, until at last he could lay a cedar log on the fire without smothering it. He rose stiffly to his feet and listened for the coyotes above the snap and crackle of the burning cedar. For a moment, all he could hear was the pounding of his own heart. Then, like spirit voices, the coyote wails seemed to come from everywhere. One howl sounded right outside the brush fence.

Reba growled. Adam looked down at her. The hair on her neck and back stood on end. She lowered her head and looked intently at the opening in the brush fence. Adam followed her gaze. Two pairs of yellow eyes glowed in the darkness just outside. The night felt suddenly very cold. His knees shook. He had forgotten to pull the brush across the opening! Quickly, he ran forward waving his arms and shouting. He grabbed at a branch of hog plum. It was hard to get a good grip on it without pricking his hands. The tough branches dug grooves into the caliche, and the sharp twigs scratched his bare legs. At last he fitted all the branches into place. He sighed with relief. There was no need to fear those yellow eyes in the blackness beyond. The mail station was now completely ringed by the brush fence.

He came back and threw another branch of cedar on the fire. Sparks flew up into the dark sky. Adam sank down on his heels and watched them. They seemed to turn into white stars high above him. How bright the Milky Way was tonight! There was the Big Dipper. With his finger, he followed out an imaginary line from the lip of the dipper and found the North Star. It glowed faintly in the dark sky just as it did back home. He found another constellation, Orion with his belt and sword of stars. Uncle Seth had pointed that out to him. Where was Cassiopeia? Ah, there she was! That was a hard one to find. Now that he thought about it, Ryansville with this same bowl of stars over it wasn't so far away after all.

Adam's knees, warmed by the fire, weren't shaking anymore. A yelp broke the quiet. He stood up and cupped his hands to his mouth: "Get away you old cowards, you hear?" The yelping stopped. He glanced around at the brush fence. It was thin in some places. He looked harder at one spot. Yes, there were yellow eyes peering in at him. He waved his arms and danced wildly toward it. "Get, you yellow cowards, get!" he yelled just as Uncle Seth had done. The eyes vanished.

19

He smiled. Uncle Seth's advice worked. These coyotes weren't too hard to handle. Pretty soon he could go to bed.

Suddenly the Plymouth Rocks began squawking loudly. They flapped down from the brush fence where they had been roosting and ran toward Adam, their barred wings held straight out from their sides, their thick red combs flopping from side to side. There was a snarl and crash. Adam looked in disbelief at the coyote scrambling over the fence toward the chickens. He ran into the tent and grabbed the Winchester, cocking it as he came out. With unsteady hands, he raised the gun and fired at the coyote. There was a spurt of flame, and the gun kicked hard against his shoulder. The coyote yelped and fell back to the other side of the fence.

The chickens had run behind the tent. Now they were squawking again. Adam heard another bark and a crash. He ran around the tent. The shadowy form was almost over the fence. He cocked the gun and fired. The spurt of flame and howl of the animal seemed to happen at the same time. The coyote fell into the yard. Reba was upon it in an instant. She growled and snapped at the dying animal.

"Get away, Reba, get away!" Adam shouted at her, but Reba wouldn't leave the coyote until it lay quite still.

Adam looked at the brush fence. It was four feet high, yet the coyotes could jump over it. His father was right—they were mighty bold. If the drouth did drive them mad, he couldn't risk being bitten by them. He would have to build the fence higher tomorrow, but tonight he must keep his gun ready to fire on these marauding animals at any moment. He could hear the Plymouth Rocks inside the tent squawking sleepily as they hunted for another roosting place. He heard the whirring flap of their wings. They must have flown up on top of something. He hoped it wasn't his bed.

Adam walked back and forth outside the tent. With the chickens out of sight and smell, the yellow eyes seemed content to wait. Were they waiting until the fire died down? Waiting until he grew too tired to hold his gun up?

Adam's eyelids felt as if there were sand under them. He blinked hard to make his eyes stay open. He counted stars for a while; then yellow eyes peering through the brush; then the pieces of firewood left on the dwindling pile. His head throbbed, and the fire seemed to pulse in and out as he watched it. The Winchester was growing heavier, too. It took all his strength to raise it to his shoulder. When would the coyotes go away? When could he go to sleep?

Wearily, Adam threw another cedar branch on the fire. He was aware now of the whimpers and snarls and padding feet that ringed the mail station. Reba stood rigid by his side. Her eyes darted from one place to another, her hair raised on her back. Growls rumbled in her throat at the strange noises outside the brush fence.

Slowly the constellations slid across the sky. A thin streak of light in the east brought the brushland out of the darkness and turned it into the shadowy shapes of low hills and mesquite trees and sagebrush. With heavy eyes, Adam watched the coyotes slink away one by one, their bushy tails held low to the ground. He let the fire die down.

Stiffly, he rose to his feet and pushed back the tent flap. He entered the dusky room and stood the Winchester in the corner. The hens had gone to roost on top of the supplies. Their feathers were puffed out like pillows. Their heads were tucked under their wings. Thank goodness, they weren't on his bed. With a shuddering sigh, Adam plunked onto the cot and sank into a deep sleep.

2

ADAM was faintly aware of barking when he awoke. At first it seemed far way, then very near, almost in his ears. He turned his head and opened his eyes. Reba stood beside the cot, rump up, shoulders down, barking furiously, her nose pointed at the supplies. Adam raised himself on his elbow and tried to focus his eyes, still full of sleep. The tip of a dust-colored tail was disappearing under the lid of the skillet which leaned against the flour sack. Adam rolled back on the bed. Just another horned toad, no doubt.

He reached over and slapped the dog on the back. "Reba! Hush up! You're hurtin' my ears!" Reba turned. She jumped up on top of Adam, her mouth open in a wide grin, her tail wagging. Joyfully she licked at his face. Adam turned his head to escape her wet kisses and pushed at her sturdy paws planted in his middle. "Get off my stomach, you old hound!" he said laughing. Reba jumped off the cot, and Adam sat up.

The air was hot and stifling in the little tent. There was the strange odor of pepper and vinegar and cucumbers. It must be the smell of the canvas when the sun beat on it, Adam thought. He could smell coffee beans and chickens, too, but he knew where *those* smells came from! He climbed slowly out of bed and shuffled through the tent opening. He shaded his eyes for a moment from the sudden bright glare, then squinted up at the sun. It must be around ten o'clock. Had he slept that long?

His mouth felt dry, and his body was sticky with sweat. He trudged around to the shade on the north side of the tent, where his father had rolled the water barrel the day before. Water, oozing from its seams, trickled down the sides and formed a damp ring on the caliche. A long-handled tin dipper lay on the barrel's wooden top. Adam lifted the lid and dipped deep. He leaned over and drank. The water trickled from the dipper onto the ground and splattered muddy yellow drops on his bare feet. It felt cool. He dipped again into the barrel and, leaning farther over, poured the dipperful over his head. He caught his breath as the water cascaded around his ears and over his face and dripped from the end of his nose. He lifted his shirttail and wiped his face, then ran his fingers through his damp hair. There was that curious smell of cucumbers again. It must be he was hungry.

Juanita had packed a big tin box of homemade biscuits the day before. They were in the tent on top of the supplies now. These would have to serve as his breakfast, he decided. It was getting late, and he needed to find game of some kind for his father's dinner. Adam went into the tent, stuffed some biscuits into his pockets,

24

and reloaded the Winchester. When he came out, he threw a biscuit to Reba. She caught it in mid-air. "Good girl!" he exclaimed, and patted her on the head. The Plymouth Rocks were clucking in the shade of the brush fence. Adam crumpled a biscuit in his hands and threw it toward them. The hens scrambled forward, eagerly pecking at the crumbs.

He pushed the brush aside and headed for the tank. It would be hard to find any game this late in the morning, but maybe a few quail were still feeding in the dry buckwheat. Heat waves shimmered ahead of him. Far down the trail, they looked almost like water. He called Reba to stay beside him. Together, they wandered past paloverdes with their yellow-green bark, past squat prickly pear cactus with their oblong green pads, past dried stalks of sotol curving out of their bushy crowns of saw-toothed leaves. They skirted gaunt gray skeletons of cholla. Adam remembered that Uncle Seth had a chair at his house made from these filigreed cactus stalks. They passed a stand of feathery mesquite trees, whose long pods, dangling from the limbs, made shadows on the ground like dark cracks in dry mud.

It was almost an hour before Adam spotted a covey of quail motionless beneath the shade of a scrub cedar. He aimed carefully and fired. There was an explosion of feathers, a whirr of frightened wings, and two birds flopped on the ground. Adam looked up anxiously at the sun. It was getting close to noon. Two quail were not enough for a meal. He should hunt more. But he had to get back to the station if he expected to have

dinner ready when his father arrived. He wished he hadn't slept so late.

He hurried back with the quail. He was able to start the fire quickly from last night's coals, but it took longer than he had figured to pick the tiny feathers from the birds. He cleaned them and put them in the skillet. They looked so little in the big kettle. How could he stretch them? He guessed he'd have to stew them and make gravy. Adam took the skillet around to the water barrel and poured several dippers full of water over the quail. He remembered the tin of biscuits. If he poured the gravy over the biscuits, that should be filling. He sprinkled a little salt on the birds, set the skillet over the fire, and went into the tent for the lid.

Reba had pushed ahead of him. Now she was growling, the hair upright on her back. Adam looked down at her. She was stalking the skillet lid. He remembered the dusty creature he had seen slide under it earlier. "What's the matter, Reba? Another hornytoad?" Adam smiled. He reached down for the lid. He could smell cucumbers again. There was a loud buzzing as if an enormous bee were caught in a kettle. Adam paused and listened. Reba was snapping and growling at the lid. The buzz came again. Adam's hand was almost on the handle when he realized what was making the sound. He drew back quickly. It wasn't a horned toad under that lid. It was a rattlesnake!

Adam backed out of the tent. What should he do? He didn't dare use the gun. The bullet might crack the skillet lid. He glanced about. The ax he had used the night before lay beside the spade outside the tent. He picked the ax up and went inside. Now to knock the lid over so the snake wouldn't strike. Reba was still snapping at it. "Get away, Reba! Get away!" Adam seized her by the tail and pulled her back. Her paws made reluctant grooves in the dirt. Cautiously, Adam reached forward and flipped the lid over with the ax blade.

There lay a large yellowish-gray rattler with dusty diamond markings overlapping down its back. With its flattened head taut against its coiled body, it fastened black bead-eyes on Adam. Its forked tongue darted in and out, while the buttons above the sharp white band at the end of its tail blurred in a warning rattle. Adam lifted the ax and brought it down with all his might. There was a loud crunch. The writhing snake's body hit the skillet lid and sent it skidding under the cot. Adam lifted the ax blade high and struck again. The snake's head lay motionless in the dirt, while the thick coils of its body wound back and forth upon each other. With the ax blade, Adam knocked the head out through the tent opening and flipped it into the campfire. He went back, slid the ax handle under the snake's body, carried it outside, and laid it beside that of the coyote near the brush fence.

Returning to the tent, he went down on his knees and pulled the lid from under the bed. He put it on the skillet. The quail bubbled and steamed over the fire. He glanced at the sun again. Time certainly passed quickly; he had better grind the coffee beans.

With the quail cooking, Adam hung the coffeepot by its hook from a metal rod held up over the fire by two side supports. He thought once more of the brush fence. He remembered the mesquite trees he had seen that morning. Their thorny branches would be just right to build up the fence. The trees weren't very far from camp. Maybe while the dinner cooked, he could chop one down.

He had just cut through the trunk and was wiping his hot face on his shirt sleeve when he saw a thin tan-colored feather of dust rising from the brushland to the north. It was coming toward him. He realized it must be his father. Adam glanced toward the south. There was a twin feather, farther away, coming from that direction, too. That must be Uncle Seth. Adam picked up the ax and ran toward the camp. He arrived only a few minutes before his father.

In a choking cloud of yellow dust, Joe Vance brought the wagon to a halt. The horses stamped their thick hoofs and tossed their wet manes. They stood before the opening in the brush fence, their dusty harnesses creaking rhythmically as their sweaty chests heaved for air.

Adam's father leaned a big hand on the wagon seat and vaulted to the ground. "Well, Son, how are things goin'? I see the coyotes didn't get you last night." He took his hat off and whacked it against his knee. A puff of yellow dust rose from it. Beads of perspiration stood out on his forehead, pale where the hatband had covered it. Below his forehead his face was leathery-tan from wind and sun. He pulled a large red handkerchief from his hip pocket and wiped at the sweat. "What you doin' with that ax?" he said.

Adam looked down at it. "Gettin' some more brush for the fence. It wasn't high enough."

His father looked questioningly at him. "High enough for what?"

Adam was reluctant to answer. "High enough to keep the coyotes out last night."

Joe caught sight of the dead coyote by the fence. "You shoot that one?"

"Yep," Adam answered.

Joe Vance walked over and poked the animal with the scuffed toe of his dusty boot. A swarm of bluebottle flies rose and settled on the hog plum branches. "Why'd you drag him in here?" he asked.

Adam looked at his father in surprise. "I didn't drag him in here! That's right where I shot him. He jumped clean over the fence tryin' to get at the hens."

His father shook his head. "I was afraid somethin' like this might happen."

"Only two tried to climb over, and I got both of them," Adam hastily added. "The rest scared easy. I did just like Uncle Seth said—hollered and waved my arms —and they went away." He didn't dare mention how frightened he had been.

Joe Vance put his hat back on his head and turned toward the tent. "See you got a rattler, too. Looks like you've been pretty busy. Better bury those carcasses pretty soon." He walked around the corner.

Adam hurried to the fire. He wadded his shirttail up for a potholder and lifted the skillet lid. The quail bobbing about in the boiling water didn't look very well cooked. But he knew he'd have to make the gravy now. He brought the flour sack from the tent and dumped a little into the skillet. He stirred it around. Big sticky gray lumps began to bob about with the quail. It didn't look like gravy at all! He tasted it. It was flat and pasty and needed lots more salt. He went into the tent and brought out the saltbox and tin of biscuits. At least Juanita's homemade biscuits were good, and the coffee was beginning to smell as it should.

Dust drifted across the camp, and Adam looked up to see Uncle Seth reining his team to a stop. He climbed out of his wagon and sauntered over to the fire. Adam's face was scarlet from the heat, and his dark hair stuck to his sweaty forehead. He glanced up and smiled briefly. His uncle grinned back, pushed his hat to the rear of his head, and crouched on his heels beside Adam. He peered at the tiny birds anchored to the skillet now by the thick gummy gravy. "Don't tell me you bagged a couple of quail! Why, that's my favorite dish!"

There was a loud hissing, and clouds of steam rose. The coffee had boiled over into the fire. Uncle Seth pulled his big red handkerchief from his pocket and lifted the coffeepot from the hook. "You need a couple of extra hands here," he smiled.

Joe Vance came out of the tent with two tin cups and plates. "Dish it up, Son! We'll have to eat now."

Adam placed a quail on each plate and spooned

the lumpy gravy over the biscuits. He filled the two tin cups with coffee.

Joe Vance reached out and handed a plate to his brother. "Let's hunker down in the tent shade," he said.

Adam watched them eat. He could tell the quail was tough by the way his father twisted the carcass back and forth to pull it apart. His father looked up. "Better go water the horses, Adam," he said.

The boy unhitched his father's team first and led them to the tank. Their big hoofs made sucking sounds when they crossed the sticky yellow ground near the pond. Adam walked into the water with them. His feet sank into the cool slippery mud that oozed up between his toes. Little puffs of yellow sediment clouded the water with each step. The sun sparkled on the crisscrossing ripples that fanned out from the splashing legs of the horses. Adam watched the water string down from the horses' mouths as they lifted their heads from their cooling drink. They didn't want to leave the tank, but Adam pulled and tugged and soon had them plodding along the hot dusty path back to camp.

He had taken Uncle Seth's team down to the tank and back when his father came over and jumped up into his wagon. Adam watched his father's muscles bulge as he heaved the heavy canvas mailbag over into Uncle Seth's wagon. He wished he could be as strong and big as his father. Maybe, someday, he would be. Uncle Seth climbed into his own wagon and threw the mailbag he had brought from Rio Verde over into Adam's father's wagon. Adam hitched his father's team to the traces and was walking around to Seth's wagon when his father called.

"Adam, come here a minute."

He ran back. His father had climbed over into the wagon seat and was adjusting the reins. He looked down at Adam. "That quail was a mite tough. Guess you didn't cook it long enough."

Adam hung his head. "I know it, Pa."

Joe Vance leaned toward his son. "If you're goin' to take care of this station for me, you've got to remember the cookin' comes first."

Adam nodded, and drew a circle in the dust with his right foot.

"I'm still not sure I'm doin' the right thing to leave you here with nothin' but rattlers and coyotes for company, Son. And if havin' a meal ready on time is too much for you, then for sure I'll have to get someone older." He leaned over to pat his son's shoulder. "Try to manage your mornin's better after this." He slapped the reins on the horses' flanks, and the mail wagon rolled away, pulling a cloud of yellow dust after it.

A lump was beginning to form in Adam's throat. He turned to help Uncle Seth with his team, but Uncle Seth had already finished, and had climbed into the wagon seat. He turned his team around.

Adam looked up at him. "I'm sorry those quail were so tough, Uncle Seth."

His uncle smiled down at him. "Don't pay it any mind, Adam. Takes a little while to get used to cookin' over a campfire again." He clucked to his team, the harnesses creaked, and the wagon rolled away towards Rio Verde.

Adam stood and watched the two clouds of dust trail in opposite directions. His first meal had been a failure. If only he could have told his father all the things that had happened. But he didn't want to tell him. If he did, his father might think it was too dangerous for him to stay, and get someone else. Adam walked slowly back over the hard caliche to the fire, burned down to white coals.

He reached over and dipped a biscuit into the gravy left in the bottom of the skillet and munched disconsolately. It was hard to swallow with that lump in his throat. He wiped his sleeve across his eyes. Reba came over and laid her chin on his knees. Her eyes pleaded. "Oh, all right, you old pot-licker!" Adam dipped another biscuit in the gravy and watched the dog eat greedily.

A shadow glided swiftly across the tent, over the fire, and disappeared beyond the brush fence. Adam looked up. It was that turkey buzzard again. This time he knew why it was here. He must bury the coyote and the snake. Adam picked up the shovel lying beside the tent and went around to the dead coyote. He dragged it by its bushy tail out through the opening in the brush fence, and off to the lee side of the station. Reba followed in the smooth path left behind it. She sniffed at the ticked fur. When Adam returned for the snake, he cut the rattles off. There were only five buttons. It wasn't such a big snake after all.

34

With the coyote and the snake buried, Adam turned his attention to the brush fence. He went back to the mesquite tree and chopped at the branches. The day was so hot he wished he could wait till evening, but he knew that the fence must be done by then. Big red ants scurried across the heated ground, stopping now and then to pick up a seed or fallen bug. Adam dragged a mesquite branch through one of their mounds by mistake. He had to abandon the branch when the twigs suddenly swarmed with angry swaying fighters whose bites felt like tiny red coals laid against his skin.

It was well toward evening when Adam hoisted the last mesquite branch onto the brush. The fence was six feet high all around now, and he had plugged the thin places with more branches. There was a big pile of firewood near the tent, too. Tired and hot, he remembered the cool tank. There was no one around to say he couldn't go in.

He scuffed down the dusty path, over the sticky mud, and waded out into the water, clothes and all. He ducked under the murky surface and stood up gasping. His pants pockets sagged with muddy water and his shirt clung to his body, but he was cool! Cool! He splashed water at Reba who barked at him from shore, and he laughed when she shied away from the sparkling drops. When at last he started back toward the camp, the warm air felt soft against his skin. His wet shirt flapping about him felt cold on his back.

The sun had set over the hills to the west. Now would be a good time to hunt, he knew. Rabbits and armadillos and javelina would be out foraging. He loaded the Winchester and called Reba to him. Going back through the brush fence, they followed the path that led away from the tank. High above, the nighthawks circled again, feeding on the tiny gnats that eddied up from the tank. The mocker was singing on top of a prickly pear cactus near the cholla. The plaintive "chuck-will's-widow, chuck-will's-widow," rose in the pale air.

Adam searched the dry buckwheat and *perezia* for sudden movements. He watched the patches of limp dusty mallow. He was about to turn back when a cottontail hopped across the trail just ahead of him. He raised the gun and fired. The rabbit flipped in the air and lay jerking on the ground near the thick leaves of a yucca plant. There was a warning buzz and a streak of motion. He jumped back. A rattlesnake recoiled on the ground before him. He lifted his gun again. Dust flew up. The head of the snake disintegrated. The scaly body thrashed on the ground before him. Adam held his foot on the lower part of the body, took out his pocket knife, and cut the rattles off. He stuffed them into his pocket.

Walking around the snake, he picked up the rabbit. It was a large one and would make a good meal. He started back to camp, the Winchester over his right shoulder, the rabbit dangling by its hind legs from his left hand. He was nearing the cholla when another diamond rattler slithered across his path. It disappeared under a clump of sotol. Adam stopped and looked about. Where were all the rattlers coming from? That made three he had seen already today.

36

Holding the rabbit against him, Adam ran toward the camp. Inside the station, he whistled to Reba and laid the Winchester and the rabbit on the ground. He pulled the brush across the opening, picked up the gun and rabbit, and headed for the tent. The Plymouth Rocks were teetering on the mesquite. No need to worry about them tonight. No coyote could ever jump *that* high. Adam looked with satisfaction at his snug fence. It reminded him of a fortress wall.

He went around by the water barrel. He would dress the rabbit and put it in cold water in the skillet overnight. In the morning he would cook it. He reached in to dip water from the barrel. He could smell cucumbers again. He thought back over each time he had smelled them that day . . . this morning when Reba woke him . . . when he had reached down for the skillet lid just before he killed the rattler in the tent. Slowly it dawned on him what the scent came from.

Adam looked around at the brush fence. Despite its height, it didn't look snug any more. Why, anything could crawl through it! He laid the dipper down on top of the barrel and picked up the Winchester. He cocked it. In the dusk, forms were not too distinct; but looking down between the water barrel and tent, he saw what he knew would be there. He moved around and aimed the gun carefully. He mustn't shoot a hole in the water barrel. The gun spurted flame in the dusk. There was a loud thumping, then a thin buzz. Out from behind the water barrel surged the thick coils of another rattler.

3

THE SUN'S first rays had barely touched the tops of the mesquite when Adam was out of bed and down on his knees beside the coals of last night's fire. He raked away the powdery white ashes he had piled over them, sprinkled a handful of twigs onto them, and sat back on his heels yawning as he watched the gray pungent smoke curl upward in the quiet morning air.

A pair of crows high above him flew toward the tank with slow deliberate strokes. Their black wings glinted in the early sun. He watched them circle above the water, pale and glassy-smooth, then flap noisily down to a landing at the edge. Their loud cawing mingled with the "bob-white, bob-white" of the quail in the buckwheat, and the high frenzied shrilling of the crickets in the sotol crowns. Although Adam was just getting up, the brushland had been awake for hours.

The fire was crackling and snapping. Adam stood up, shooed the Plymouth Rocks out from under foot, and walked to the water barrel. The snake he had killed the night before lay near the fence. He squatted down and cut the rattles away. He would put these with the others which he had stuffed under his cot pad.

The covered skillet with the dressed rabbit inside sat on the barrel lid. Reba came over and lifted her nose to sniff at the meat. Adam smiled at her. "You've got to wait, Reba. That's for dinner." He poured the water out of the skillet into a pan he had placed on the ground for the chickens. They dipped their beaks down, then tilted their heads back so the cool water could trickle down their long throats. He looked about and wondered where they might have laid their eggs. He'd been so busy the last two days he hadn't had time to think about their nests. Right now, a couple of fried eggs would taste mighty good.

Skirting the brush fence, Adam peered into the hog plum and mesquite for spots on the ground large enough for the hens to nest in. He found one egg in the brush opposite the back of the tent, and another near the campfire. There should be four eggs by now. Perhaps the rattlesnakes had found the rest.

He took the rabbit out of the skillet and put it on a plate out of Reba's reach, then went back into the tent and pulled out the slab of bacon from its flour-sack covering. Slicing two thick pieces, he returned to the fire and put the skillet on. The bacon sizzled and curled slowly at the edges. Adam sat back on his haunches and closed his eyes, sniffing loudly. Was there anything that smelled better than bacon frying over a campfire? He could smell the sagebrush and creosote bushes, too. Thank goodness he didn't smell any cucumbers yet! He broke the two eggs into the skillet and watched them turn white. He liked the yolks hard.

Reba sat at his elbow while he ate, her eyes following each bite he took. "Oh, here, you old hound!" Adam held out the bacon rinds, and the dog gulped them hungrily. He crumpled up several biscuits into the bacon grease and stirred them about. That would have to be Reba's breakfast.

Rinsing the skillet out, Adam put the rabbit back into it, poured several dippers of water over it, sprinkled salt on it, and set the covered kettle on the fire. This rabbit had looked too tough to roast. It would have to be stewed. Maybe some sage leaves would make it more tasty. Adam pushed aside the brush fence and headed for the nearest sage bush.

He could see fresh coyote tracks in the dusty path. They'd been back again last night. It was a good thing he had built the fence up the day before. They had howled and yelped and padded and sniffed all around the brush, but they hadn't tried to jump over. Just as well. There wasn't much time to think about coyotes. Before he had gone to bed, he had made himself a torch and had looked carefully under his cot and around the supplies. Even this morning, before he got up, he had hung his head over the edge of his cot and checked carefully to make sure there wasn't another rattler coiled under his bed.

Adam stopped at the purple sagebrush. Its spears of dusty flowers had long since dried, but the silver-gray leaves, rough like a cat's tongue, stood stiff and leathery on the dark stalks. He selected several of the soft tender young shoots at the ends of the branches. These had the best flavor, he knew. He pinched them off with his fingernails. Returning to camp, he walked over to the fire, lifted the skillet lid, and dropped the sage leaves onto the simmering rabbit. He'd be sure to have dinner on time today, and it would be a good meal, too. If he could find another egg, maybe he could make some dumplings. His father had showed him how, last time they went camping. He walked around the brush fence again, looking more carefully this time for another egg. Ah, there was one! It was so far back he wondered how the Plymouth Rock had managed to squeeze in there. He had to get down on his knees and stretch one arm into the thorny mesquite to reach the egg.

That noon, when the two plumes of tan-colored dust trailed up to the mail station, Adam was ready. His father climbed out of the wagon seat and jumped to the ground. He turned and reached back under the seat, drawing out a large tin box. He handed it to Adam.

"Juanita made you some biscuits, and Becky sent along these cookies. She says, 'Tell Adam not to eat the cookies all at once.' "

Adam took the box and grinned. He remembered how Becky used to chase him out of the kitchen whenever she made cookies. He'd always manage to sneak his pockets full. He put the box in the tent and brought out the tin cups and plates. Lifting the skillet lid slowly, he looked with satisfaction at the fat moist dumplings steaming inside. The rabbit underneath was soft and tender and smelled richly of sage. He filled the two plates and handed them to Uncle Seth and his father. They crouched in the shade of the tent.

Uncle Seth bit into a dumpling. "Um-UM! That's larrupin' good! Adam, you can come cook at my house any time!"

Joe Vance nodded and threw a rabbit bone at Reba. "Not bad, Son. Could stand a little more salt, maybe."

Adam ran to bring his father the salt sack. Entering the tent, he caught sight of a sudden motion on the ground in front of the flour sack. The warning buzz brought him to an abrupt halt. Weaving slightly, the yellowish-gray head of a rattler drew back in the familiar S. Adam reached over for the Winchester lying on the bed. He cocked the gun, aimed, and fired.

Outside the tent, he heard his father's coffee cup clank loudly against his tin plate. "What in tarnation are you doing, Adam?"

Adam laid the gun on the bed, lifted the salt sack from the top of the supplies, and pushed out into the sunshine.

"Just shot another rattler, Pa."

His father turned and looked at Adam. "*Another* rattler!" Joe Vance wiped at the coffee he had spilled on his shirt sleeve.

Uncle Seth bit into a dumpling. "You got to expect rattlers in brushland." He looked at Adam. "How many you killed?"

Adam handed his father the salt. "I've got three

tails already—this will make the fourth."

Joe Vance looked at his brother. "Not the time of year for them to be migratin' . . . ." He turned back to Adam. "You kill them all here in the mail station?"

Adam shook his head. "Nope. I killed one just outside when I was hunting last night." He waved his arm towards the brushland. "They're all over out there."

Uncle Seth gazed at the low hills in the distance, hazy blue in the hot noon sun. "I reckon they've got their dens over yonder."

Adam followed his uncle's gaze. "What they doin' over *here*, then?"

Uncle Seth brought his eyes back to his half-empty plate. "Lookin' for quail and little rabbits. You got to expect rattlers in brushland."

Adam's father turned to Uncle Seth. "But not this many . . . . Might see one or two in a few days, maybe, but not as many as Adam has."

Uncle Seth watched Adam bring the skillet from the fire. "They're lookin' for shade . . . . Rattlers curl up anywhere it's cool."

Adam ladled a big dumpling onto Uncle Seth's plate. "You suppose they're after water at the tank?" he asked.

Uncle Seth nodded, "Sure enough could be, Adam." He took another bite and munched slowly, then slapped his knee. "I think I've got it, Adam!"

Adam looked expectantly at his uncle. "What?"

Uncle Seth shook his fork at Adam. "You're camped

square in the middle of a *rattlesnake run*, that's what!"

"A rattlesnake run?"

"Yep!" Uncle Seth picked up a rabbit leg and gnawed at the meat.

"What's a rattlesnake run, Uncle Seth?"

Adam's uncle threw the leg bone to Reba. "That's a stretch of land the snakes travel over goin' and comin'. It's like a road would be to us, only wider."

Joe Vance turned to his brother. "Then that explains it!"

"Explains what?" Uncle Seth asked.

"Why Cy Connley's men left this station—too many rattlers!"

Adam dished more rabbit onto his father's plate. "Could we move the mail station out of the run, Pa?"

"Reckon we could, but we don't want to get too far from the tank—have to water those horses, you know." Joe Vance drained his coffee cup and wiped his mustache with the back of his hand. "Which way you reckon we should go, Seth?"

Uncle Seth stood up and squinted at the hills in the west. "If their dens are over yonder and they're travelin' towards the tank, then this spot right here is dead center . . . could move the station either north or south a piece."

Adam held up the tin Becky had sent, and Uncle Seth selected a cookie. "How do you know how far to move it?" he asked.

Uncle Seth munched the cookie. "By the rattlesnake trails. When they peter out, that's the end of the run."

Adam looked puzzled. "I never saw a snake trail before. What does it look like?"

Reaching into the tin, Uncle Seth took a biscuit out. "See this? You tie a string around this biscuit and drag it in the dust, and you'll see what a snake trail looks like."

Adam waved his arms toward the brushland. "But it isn't dusty every place."

"No, but with this drouth, there's enough places where snakes could leave a trail," Uncle Seth said.

Adam's father turned to Uncle Seth. "Let's scout out another spot. Can't do much more than that today. Got to get back to town before dark."

Adam started for the tent. "Better take the Winchester in case you meet up with more rattlers."

Uncle Seth shook his head. "No need. They won't be movin' around in this sun. Like I said—they curl up in the shade where it's cool. Evenin's you got to be careful."

Joe Vance pushed the tent flap aside as he passed and looked at the dead rattlesnake on the ground. "That's a right big snake, Son. You shot his head off clean, too. Don't mess around with that head, you hear? The poison in those fangs is dangerous for a long spell after the head's cut off."

"I'll bury the snake after you leave, Pa."

"No, don't bury the body, just the head. I've been needin' some snake oil for my harnesses. You skin that

46

rattler, cut it up, and render out the oil in the skillet. Maybe you could bag a couple more. . . . Snake oil is real fine for guns, too."

Adam didn't like the idea of having to hunt more snakes. "What will I do with the oil?" he asked.

"Pour it into one of those empty biscuit tins," his father said, and he walked toward the opening in the fence. "You better go and water the horses, Adam, while Seth and I look around out yonder."

Unhitching his father's team, Adam led the horses toward the tank. He could see the tops of Uncle Seth's and his father's hats bobbing about in the brush. How wide was a rattlesnake run? he wondered. . . . Fifty feet? . . . One hundred feet? They would have to clear away the brush for another station. Adam winced at the thought of cutting more mesquite.

Adam's father and Uncle Seth were back at the wagon when Adam returned from the tank with the second team. They were talking as they exchanged the mailbags.

"When did it happen?" his father was asking.

Uncle Seth heaved the heavy canvas bag over into Joe Vance's wagon. "Yesterday evening, right after supper."

Joe Vance lowered the sack. "Who were they?"

"Couple of con men tried to swindle Ralph Cutter over at the livery stable. Sheriff Bradly threw them in the hoosegow . . . only been in there two days when they slipped their halters."

"Sheriff go after them?"

47

Uncle Seth laughed. "Yep, the sheriff and every man jack in Rio Verde was out combin' the brush for them till dark. Vanished like smoke, they did."

Adam backed the horses into place. He looked up at Uncle Seth. "You talkin' about escaped prisoners, Uncle Seth?"

Adam's uncle grinned down at him. "Just a couple of no-accounts."

Joe Vance looked worried. "They might be dangerous, you know."

"Not likely. Weren't even armed. Mighty sneaky, though. Took two horses tied out front of the hoosegow right from under Sheriff Bradly's nose."

Adam looked across the brushland. "Reckon they'll come out here?"

Uncle Seth shook his head. "Not this close to Rio Verde. Probably head south for the border."

Joe Vance shifted the mailbag about with his foot. "I don't like it."

Adam looked up at him. "Don't like what, Pa?"

"Those criminals runnin' loose, you here by yourself in a rattlesnake run. It's no place for a boy."

Adam clenched his fists. "Pa! How can I make you understand? I'm not a child any more!"

Uncle Seth smiled across at Adam. "I'll say you're not! Those dumplin's you dished up today were he-man dumplin's."

Joe Vance smiled down at Adam. "You're doin' all right on the cookin', Son." His face grew serious. "It's the other things out here . . ."

Adam put his fists on his hips. "What if I do run into a few snakes? You're movin' the station, aren't you?"

His father nodded and climbed over into the wagon seat. "It may be a few days, though. Found a spot to the south about a hundred yards that looks pretty fair . . . no snake trails, but lots of brush. We'll bring some tools and palin's tomorrow and start clearin'." He looked down critically at Adam's bare feet. "Better wear your boots, Son, when you go after those rattlers."

"I didn't bring them, Pa."

"I'll fetch them for you tomorrow. You be careful of those snake heads, you hear? And if anyone stops, don't get too friendly." He slapped the reins on the horses' backs, and the wagon wheels spun a cloud of yellow dust into the air. Adam watched the dust settle slowly on the mesquite branches.

Seth smiled down at Adam. "You keep your eyes peeled for those rattlers. Don't want to lose a good cook." His wagon rolled away with its trailing train of dust.

Adam sighed. Staying at the mail station wasn't as much fun as he thought it would be. He wished he could be on the wagon seat beside his father right now riding back to Ryansville. He'd like to forget all about brush fences and coyotes and rattlesnakes . . . but he couldn't. He crammed his hands into his pockets and kicked at the dust. Turning, he scuffed slowly toward the tent. The sun felt like fire on his neck. The brush fence, its bare branches yellow-gray with the powdery dust, didn't look like a fortress wall anymore. It looked like a prison. The smoke from the fire eddied lazily towards him. It surrounded his head, and he coughed at the smell, sharp, unpleasant, and stinging. The Plymouth Rocks sitting in the shade of the fence were kicking dust through their fluffed out feathers. Reba was stretched out behind the water barrel. All he could see was her tail, limp on the damp caliche.

Sinking down in the narrow shade of the tent, Adam put his head in his hands. He could feel the heat radiating up from the hard dusty ground in front of him. He wished he were little enough to crawl behind the water barrel, too. The high shrill of cicadas pulsed the air. It felt like sharp slivers of silver piercing his eardrums. He tried to shut it out, but he couldn't. Big tears filled Adam's eyes. He brushed at them angrily with the back of his hand. Any thirteen-year-old who could shoot coyotes when they jumped over fences or rattlers that coiled at his feet shouldn't be crying. He remembered the rattlesnake oil his father wanted. He had killed four snakes already . . . he guessed he could kill a few more. But that would have to wait until evening. Right now, he'd better eat something and try to rest.

When the nighthawks soared into the air, Adam loaded the Winchester, picked up an empty flour sack, and set out with Reba at his heels. The western hills made sharp silhouettes against the sunset. Tawny and bright, the glowing rays streaked the sky from hilltops to zenith. They threaded through wisps of feathery clouds, high and thin. A warm breeze, dank and fishy-smelling, blew from the tank across Adam's face. It rustled the dry yucca branches on their long gray stalks, and twirled the brown mesquite pods on stems that were thin and dark. Adam searched the ground before him for the long smooth snake paths that led toward the water.

At the tank, he gazed for a moment at the mirrored reflection of the sky. Every streak of gold, every wisp of cloud was there in the glassy water. A mockingbird flew low across the tank. The white tips of its wings flashed up and down, mirrored from beneath. Long concentric ripples flowed rhythmically across the glossy surface. Adam peered intently at their source. Was it a fish jumping? A large moth struggling in the water?

A small flat head emerged from the water and stretched upward a few inches. As though propelled from below, it moved placidly across the tank. He stepped forward and looked more closely. It was a snake swimming. He hadn't realized there were snakes in the tank.

He ran toward the spot where the snake was coming out of the water. It flowed forward in a straight line, head slightly raised, tail held up out of the water. Adam watched the snake leave the water. There was a row of buttons on the end of the tail . . . his first rattler of the evening. He took careful aim.

Adam had hardly finished stuffing the snake into the flour sack when he saw another one sliding toward the tank. He aimed and fired, but the bullet only kicked up a puff of dirt ahead of the snake. The rattler coiled at once. Its flat head drew into the S-curve that meant it was ready to strike. Adam shot again and missed. The snake lunged forward toward the spot where the dust still hung in the air. Adam aimed again. This time he hit his mark, and another writhing body lumped the sides of the flour sack. The sack was so full there was hardly space to hold the top together with his hand.

Adam started back toward camp with the flour sack over his shoulder. The snakes' bodies, coiling and uncoiling in the sack, shifted his shirt back and forth across his back. He shivered and swung the bag to the ground. He would drag it instead. But it was hard to hold the gun, drag the sack, and still keep an eye on the path ahead. He stopped and shifted the sack onto his shoulder.

There was a loud hissing buzz just to his left. Dropping the sack, he cocked his gun. Before he could aim at the coiled diamond rattler, it streaked forward, striking the sack at his feet. He jumped back. The snake's fangs had caught in the cloth, and it struggled to free itself. Adam aimed and fired.

He lowered the smoking gun and looked at the torn flour sack spilling a tangle of snakes over the path. A shiver ran through him again. How could he carry all of them back to camp? Reba came forward. Warily, she sniffed and barked at the curling bodies. Adam stooped down and pulled one of the rattlers out by the tail. "Here, Reba, you carry this one." Reba backed away. Adam advanced toward her. "Come on, girl, it can't hurt you." The dog leaned forward on braced feet and sniffed. Adam grabbed Reba's jaw, opened it, and stuck the snake's body into her mouth. She stood holding the snake and looking up at Adam. He patted her on the head. "Good girl. Good Reba! Now let's go."

Adam picked up the other two snakes by their tails and, holding them in one hand, he hoisted the Winchester to his shoulder. The snakes coiled and uncoiled as they trailed in the dust behind him. He looked back. "Come on, Reba, that's a good girl." The dog trotted forward. The snake's tail dangled out of one side of her mouth, the upper body out of the other side. When he entered the camp, Reba didn't want to give up the snake at first. She danced about with Adam after her. But at last she let him pull the scaly body from her mouth. He cut the rattles off and put them with the others under his cot pad.

Although he had never skinned a snake before, Adam had cleaned a catfish. He soon had big smooth rounds of rattler ready for the skillet, more than would fill it. He laid them aside to render out the next morning. With the fire glowing again, Adam put the skillet near the edge where it would not be too hot. It took a slow heat to render out the fat, he knew.

The sky was growing dark. Adam walked over to pull the brush fence together for the night. He drew the last branch of mesquite into place. Out of the corner of his eye, Adam caught a flash of light. He paused and looked across the brushland. It was over in the direction of Rio Verde. He saw it again. It was yellow, bright, and flickering. It reflected against a thick curl of smoke rising above it. A campfire!

Adam felt a happy surge of relief. He wasn't alone in the brushland any more. Someone else was camping out there. He wished he could meet him. It would be so pleasant to sit by a campfire and talk to someone. He wondered who the stranger might be. Maybe he was a rancher out looking for stock that had strayed down into the brushland. Maybe he was a traveler on his way to Ryansville.

Then Adam felt his happiness drain away. A knot of fear was beginning to form in his stomach. Maybe it wasn't a friend at all. Maybe it was the two men Uncle Seth had been talking about that afternoon—the ones who'd escaped from the Rio Verde jail!

4

WHEN ADAM pulled the fence aside next morning just before dawn, blue shadows covered the brushland like dark water. The mockingbird was quiet. So were the nighthawks. Only the endless chirping of crickets, slower now in the cool morning air, broke the stillness that surrounded the mail station.

A sharp smell of creosote rose from the bushes as Adam passed with his Winchester on his shoulder and Reba trotting at his heels. He peered carefully at the path just ahead of him. There were few snakes about— perhaps because it was cooler, he thought. There hadn't seemed to be many coyotes around the station last night, either. Maybe he was getting used to them. Right now there must be javelina feeding near the tank. This was the best time to hunt for them. He remembered the wild pig his father had roasted on the camping trip last summer, and licked his lips.

He paused behind a mesquite tree near the edge of the tank. Reba sat down beside him and sniffed the air, her head raised, her eyes half closed. Across the tank over the low ledge of limestone, Adam could see a clump of scrub cedar, and beneath them, dark shadows. Were they moving, or was it something else? Still too dark to tell, Adam listened intently. There was a low rustling, and then an unmistakable grunt. Javelina!

Adam cocked his gun. In the quiet air, the loud click startled him. He hoped it hadn't alerted the wild pigs under the cedar. He stood still for a moment longer. It was too dark to shoot across the tank with accuracy. He had better move around a little closer where he could see the javelina more clearly. He mustn't get too close, though, for javelina were tricky. He remembered what his father had told him last summer—sometimes the whole herd would charge a person, whether you shot at them or not.

Adam moved slowly, behind a clump of hog plum, then crouched low behind a sage bush. Reba padded and paused behind him. The sky was turning pale turquoise in the east. In the thin light, he could make out a herd of eight javelina. They were small ones. Three were lying on the cedar needles, four were rooting close by, and the lookout stood gazing across the tank. Adam decided he would shoot at the standing one. He dropped down on one knee and aimed carefully. He mustn't miss. The gun sounded like a cannon blast in the still air. The pigs squealed wildly and scrambled to their feet. Hoofs thudded. Adam jumped up and held his breath. Would they charge him? He glanced about for the nearest mesquite tree to climb into. When he looked back, the herd had melted into the brushland, except for the animal he had shot. Its dark shape lay still under the scrub cedar. Adam sighed with relief.

Reba ran ahead of him and sniffed excitedly at the young boar. It was bigger than he first realized, over two feet long. The coarse hair covering its body was a grizzled black and gray with an indistinct line of white like a collar circling its neck. Adam wondered how the tiny legs with their sharp hoofs could hold up such a thick body. In the half-opened jaws, he could see the flat razor-sharp teeth that made the javelina so dangerous. Adam laid down his gun and heaved the wild pig to his shoulder. It was heavy. He bent his knees, picked up the gun with his free hand, and started back to camp. Reba jumped beside him, her sharp barks cutting the morning quietness into noisy pieces. Adam stumbled against her as she danced across his path.

"Watch out or I'll step on you, you old hound! And hush up! No need to carry on so. You'll get a good meal directly."

Back in camp, he started the fire and put bacon in the skillet for his breakfast. The sun's first shafts of light were lancing through the brushland. They caught in the curling smoke of the campfire and turned it into a translucent cloud. From the corner of his eye, Adam caught the flashing tips of a mockingbird's wings as it flew to its perch in the cholla. He sat back a moment and listened to its clear notes purling the air. Why was it the fears that filled him at night always seemed to melt away in the morning? For some reason he felt bigger now. Maybe he had grown a little during the night.

With breakfast over, he rinsed the skillet out and dumped in more rounds of rattler he had prepared the night before. He set them on the edge of the fire where the oil would fry out slowly. Now he must dress the pig. Carefully, he skinned the carcass, making sure to cut the scent gland out of its back as his father had shown him, so it wouldn't taint the meat. The pig was awkward and heavy to handle. Adam poured dippers of water over the cleaned carcass while Reba gobbled greedily at the entrails.

He walked to the campfire and lifted the metal crossbar from the supports. He would skewer the pig on this. He had to tie the javelina securely in place with some clothesline rope to keep it from slipping around when he turned it over the fire. Carefully, he lifted the trussed carcass and placed it between the metal supports. He stepped back and smiled with satisfaction. Uncle Seth and his father would really be surprised today. And after a good meal, they would start clearing a new place for the mail station outside the rattlesnake run.

Several hours later as the sun grew hotter, Adam put more mesquite on the fire. He glanced up. It must be near nine o'clock. The pig should be nicely roasted by noon. He poured the snake oil into an empty biscuit tin and placed the skillet back on the fire.

Suddenly Reba, lying in the shade of the tent, lifted her head and growled. She stood up rumbling in her throat. Adam glanced about the camp. He couldn't see any snakes. Then he caught sight of a cloud of dust moving toward the mail station. It was coming from the direction in which he had seen the campfire the night before. The single cloud became a double cloud as it drew closer.

Adam could see two men riding side by side. His heart beat faster. Were these friendly visitors, or could they be the escaped prisoners Uncle Seth had talked about? He glanced around the camp again. He must keep the Winchester close by, but out of sight. He walked to the tent, laid the gun on the bed, and threw the edge of the quilt over it.

With a creak of saddle leather and murmured "whoas," the dusty riders drew up at the opening in the brush fence. One man, tall and thin, slouched forward, his hands on the saddlehorn, his battered felt hat tilted forward shading small eyes in an unshaven face. He darted a quick glance at the tent, the cackling hens, the campfire. Then he saw Adam. Wrinkles of surprise creased his forehead, and his hat rose slightly with the movement. "Well! I'll be! Just a tad!"

His companion, a portly man in a faded vest and frayed frock coat, turned and winked at the thin man. His voice was low. "I'll handle this, Slate," he said. He removed his dusty black hat and held it against his large chest. His bald head glistened in the hot sun. He turned to Adam. His eyes curved into an ingratiating smile in his smooth fat face. His voice was hearty now. "Good morning, young man. Allow me to introduce myself: Henry Dugan at your service . . . and my friend here, Brian Slate. Would your daddy be about?"

Adam hesitated a moment before he shook his

head. "No, sir," he said.

Dugan leaned forward. "Then your mother?"

Adam shook his head again. "She's dead, sir."

Dugan's face sagged with mock sadness. "Poor boy, poor boy!" Then his eyes lit up questioningly. "Are you all by yourself?"

Adam nodded.

Quickly the two men swung out of their saddles and, tying their horses to the mesquite tree just outside the station, strode through the dust into the camp.

Reba growled menacingly. Adam put a restraining hand on the dog. "Hush up, Reba," he commanded.

The men walked toward the campfire. They looked hungrily at the pig roasting on the spit and the rattle-snake rounds sizzling in the skillet.

Dugan turned to Adam, smiling again. "My companion and I would be most obliged to you if you could spare a bite of breakfast."

Adam knew he couldn't refuse food to a traveler. "The pig isn't done, sir, but I have some biscuits." He turned and entered the tent. Quickly, he reached for the tin box on top of the supplies. He could hear the two men talking rapidly. He strained his ears to hear what they were saying, but they had lowered their voices. With the biscuit tin under his arm, he pushed back the tent flap and glanced out. He saw Dugan reach into his pocket and pull out a pearl-handled penknife. The blade glinted in the sun as he opened it. Leaning over, Dugan speared a round of rattlesnake, blew on it, and popped it into his mouth.

Adam stepped forward to protest, but Dugan turned and smiled at him. "Excellent fish, young man, excellent fish. Didn't think they grew this big in that tank out yonder. If I didn't know it, I'd say it tasted almost like chicken." He chewed with obvious relish.

Adam wanted to laugh out loud, but he dared not. Maybe these strangers wouldn't think it was funny if they knew they were eating rattlesnake meat. Slate had pulled out a pocket knife and helped himself, too.

He wiped the grease off his stubbly chin with the back of his hand. "You say you got some biscuits?" he asked.

Adam opened the tin and held it out. Both men reached in. They munched noisily. Dugan peered into the tin again, and his face lit up. "Well now, do my eyes deceive me, or are those sugar cookies you are so generously offering me?"

Adam had forgotten the cookies in the bottom of the tin. "They're cookies, sir. My sister made them for me."

Dugan took a cookie and chewed with his eyes half closed. "Excellent cook, excellent!" His eyes popped open and looked suspiciously at the tent, then at Adam. "Your sister—here in camp with you?"

Adam shook his head. "No, sir, she's back in Ryansville."

"All by yourself, you say?"

Slate reached for another biscuit and jerked his head at the roasting pig. "Shoot that yourself?"

Adam set the biscuit tin down and put more mesquite on the fire. "Yes sir."

Slate took a big bite. "What kind of gun you got?"

Adam hesitated.

"I said what kind of gun you got?"

".44 Winchester," Adam answered.

Slate nodded and glanced at Dugan with a wink. "Kind of a big gun for a little tad like you."

Adam hooked his thumbs in his pockets. "I can handle it."

Slate narrowed his eyes. "What you doin' out here all by yourself?"

Adam pulled himself up tall. "I'm in charge of this mail station."

Slate grinned and pushed his hat back. "*You* in charge?" He laughed and turned to his companion. "Hear that, Dugan? *He's* in charge."

Dugan's round face lifted in a forced smile. "He's a mighty smart lad, Slate, that's why."

Slate rubbed his chin and glanced at the tent. "Reckon you got extra grub. We need some."

Adam looked at Slate with suspicion. "How come you're traveling out here without supplies?"

Slate's eyes darkened, and he leaned menacingly toward Adam. "Say, you're kind of big for your britches, aren't you, askin' questions that way?"

Dugan cleared his throat and laid a warning hand on Slate's arm. He turned to Adam. "You see, son, we had some . . . ah . . . urgent business to attend to, and we didn't have time to stock up. You *could* spare a little flour and coffee now, couldn't you?"

62

By now Adam was sure these were the two outlaws Uncle Seth had talked about the day before. If he could stall them off for another hour, Uncle Seth and his father would be here. These strangers weren't wearing any guns that he could see. It shouldn't be hard for his father and uncle to capture them.

He walked over and gave the spitted pig a turn. "I've got some food you can take, but why don't you wait and have dinner with me first? This javelina is more than I can eat."

Dugan beamed at him with surprise. "Why, that's right neighborly of you, young man, right neighborly!" He strolled over to the fire and gave the carcass another turn. Trickles of fat ran down its sides and fell into the fire. With each sizzling drop, a little puff of white smoke rose suddenly from the glowing coals.

Slate took his hat off and wiped his forehead with a dirty red handkerchief. "Haven't got time." He glanced at Adam. "Where's your water barrel?"

Adam waved to the shady side of the tent. "Over yonder."

Slate crossed the shimmering caliche to the water barrel. He seized the dipper, lifted the lid, and dipped deep. Water spilled over the dipper's sides as he drank thirstily. With a loud swallow, Slate smacked his lips and heaved the last drops in the dipper at Reba. The dog jumped aside. Slate wiped his hand across his wet mouth and shuffled around to the front of the tent. He lifted the tent flap and peered inside.

Adam held his breath. Would Slate see the gun

under the rumpled quilt? He had to draw Slate away from the tent. Adam looked at the horses tied to the mesquite outside, then over at the fire. With his back toward Adam, Dugan was turning the spitted pig again. Quickly, Adam stooped and picked up a stick of firewood. He tossed it lightly over the brush fence so it would land near the horses. There was a sudden loud neighing and stamping of hoofs. Slate jerked his head out of the tent.

Dugan straightened. "Go check those horses, Slate," he barked. "Might be a rattlesnake!"

Slate ran out the gate and seized the reins of the excited horses.

Adam hurried over and stood in front of the tent. He tried to make conversation so the men wouldn't be suspicious. "You camped over yonder in the direction of Rio Verde, didn't you? Thought I saw your campfire last night."

Dugan looked from Slate back to Adam. He put his hands behind his back and rocked on his heels. "Why, ah, yes, we did. . . . We saw your fire, too . . . thought we'd come over here and visit last night, but those pesky coyotes wouldn't leave us alone."

Adam smiled to himself. So *that's* where the coyotes were last night! Thank goodness for the coyotes! He nodded his head. "Yes, sir, they're mighty bold out here. Pa says it's the drouth."

Slate came back through the gate. "Nothin' out there. Those fool horses would jump at their own shadow!" He walked over beside Dugan and pulled the penknife from his pocket again. He pared at his fingernails. "When the mail wagons comin' in here?" he asked.

Adam squinted up at the sun's position. It must be near eleven o'clock. "Oh, they don't come in for a long spell yet," he lied.

Slate sniffed at the tantalizing smell of roasting pig. "Appears to me that critter's done." He reached forward with his knife to cut some of the meat away.

Adam hurried toward the fire, keeping himself between Slate and the tent. "Oh, no, sir, it isn't cooked near long enough yet . . . has to roast till noon, at least!"

Dugan nodded and turned toward Slate. "Why don't you go water the horses at the tank over yonder? Might quiet them down." He smiled at Adam. "We'll get dinner ready, won't we, son?"

"Oh, yes, sir!"

Slate snapped his knife shut. He glanced at the tent. "I say we get the grub together and pull out of here."

Dugan reached over and turned the pig once more. He looked back at Slate. Adam could see his eyes were hard although his lips were smiling. "We'll eat first, Slate. No need to disappoint this young man who has so graciously invited us to dinner."

Adam stepped back toward the tent. "That's right, sir, you take your time waterin' the horses, and I'll make some coffee. We'll have a meal ready when you get back."

Slate hesitated a moment, then turned and ambled

over to the horses. He mounted one, and taking the reins of the other, wheeled them around and headed for the tank.

Adam glanced anxiously to the north. He wished his father would hurry. If he could get Dugan and Slate to eating, maybe they wouldn't notice the dust trail from the mail wagon. He hated to feed them any of his father's dinner, but it was the only way. Going to the tent he brought out the coffee grinder, coffee beans, and pot.

Dugan sniffed audibly at the aroma of fresh coffee which arose from the whirring grinder, while Adam turned the crank. Reaching down, Dugan picked up the pot. "Here, my lad, let me fill this." He walked to the water barrel and carefully ladled dippers of water into the pot, then brought it back to Adam. Adam poured the ground coffee into a cotton salt sack, tied the open end, and dropped the bag into the coffeepot, then hung the pot over the coals. Dugan rubbed his chubby hands together in anticipation.

The coffee was steaming fragrantly when Slate trotted the horses back from the tank. He dismounted, tied them to the mesquite, and strode toward the campfire. Dugan was turning the roast pig. Beads of sweat stood out on his upper lip, and his cheeks were flushed from the fire. He was licking his fat lips as he watched the meat turn a golden brown.

Adam was walking out of the tent with the cups and plates when he saw the familiar feather of dust rising to the north. He stopped short. His father was com-

67

ing at last!

Slate glanced over at Adam. "What you starin' at?" he asked.

Adam started. He had almost given away his father's approach. "Oh, nothin', sir, nothin' at all. Here, Mr. Slate, you sit over here . . . I'll get you a nice piece of roast meat." Adam tried to steer Slate around so his back would be toward the north, but Slate's eyes narrowed and he looked intently around the horizon. He saw the dust cloud, too.

Turning, Slate seized Adam's arm. "I thought you said the mail wagon didn't get here till later."

Adam's arm hurt in the fierce grip. "I did! I did!"

Dugan looked up. "What's this?"

Slate dropped Adam's arm and pushed him toward the tent. "Now get that grub for us, you hear? And the gun, too!"

Dugan walked quickly over to Slate. "See here! There's no need to get rough with the boy. He can get the supplies for us after we've eaten."

"We're not eatin'!" Slate pointed to the north. "See that dust? It's the mail wagon comin' in. We've got to get out of here fast!"

Dugan squinted at the dust cloud growing nearer every minute. "By George, you're right, Slate!" He turned and hurried toward the fire. "Just let me cut off a side of this roast, first."

Slate grabbed Dugan's coattails and pulled him back. "Forget it, Dugan! There isn't time!"

Dugan looked longingly at the roasting javelina,

68

then at the approaching dust cloud. He turned reluctantly toward the horses.

Adam stood between the men and the tent, the cups and plates still in his hands. Slate hurried toward the tent. He pushed Adam roughly aside. Adam swung at Slate's head, catching him just behind the ear with one of the tin cups.

Slate wheeled around, "Why you little —!" He grabbed Adam by the shoulders and threw him to the ground. The cups and plates clattered in all directions. Reba rushed in barking and snapped at Slate's heels.

It was Dugan's turn now. He seized Slate's arm and hauled him toward the horses. Slate, kicking at the dog, tried to yank free from Dugan.

"The gun, Dugan, we got to get the gun!"

Dugan's eyes were hard. "Not now. Can't you see this smart brat has stalled us until it's too late? Come on!"

Adam could hear the thud of hoofs and the rattle of the approaching mail wagon.

Slate heard them, too. He ran toward the horses, with Dugan right behind him. They mounted quickly, kicked their ponies into a gallop, and headed east in a cloud of yellow dust.

Adam sat up and rubbed his hands on his jeans. His plan to hold the outlaws until his father arrived had *almost* worked. At least they hadn't taken the gun or supplies . . . nor the dinner, either, come to think of it!

5

Adam was still on the ground when his father pulled up at the mail station. Joe Vance leaped from the wagon, tied the horses, and ran toward his son. Adam could see deep furrows between his father's eyes. His voice sounded almost shaky. "You all right, Adam?"

Adam got quickly to his feet, dusting his pants. "Sure, Pa."

Joe Vance brushed the thick caliche powder from Adam's back. "I started racin' the horses soon as I saw that cloud of dust leavin' the mail station. Who was it?"

"Those two jailbreakers from Rio Verde that Uncle Seth told us about yesterday."

Joe Vance stopped brushing and looked intently into Adam's face. "You sure?"

"Pretty sure, Pa. They wanted the gun and food supplies, but I stalled them off till they saw you comin'."

Adam could see the muscles in his father's face work in and out. "Were they armed?"

"I didn't see any guns."

70

"Did they get the Winchester?"

Adam shook his head. "I hid it under the quilts when I saw them comin'."

Adam's father patted him on the back of the neck. "Smart thinkin', Son! Which way did they go?"

Adam pointed to the east. "That way. Only you can't see their dust now."

Adam's father shaded his eyes with his hand and looked out over the brushland. "Probably stopped in an arroyo somewhere." Adam could see those same face muscles work in and out again. "If that doesn't beat all!" Joe Vance took his hat off and shook his head. He slapped the hat against the side of his leg. "I *knew* I shouldn't have left you out here by yourself!"

Adam bent over and picked up a cup. He dusted it out with his shirttail. "They weren't too bad, Pa. They didn't hurt me any!"

"Why were you on the ground then?"

"Slate tried to get into the tent, so I hit him with a cup and he knocked me down. Then he heard you comin' and lit out for his horse."

"Slate? Slate who?"

"Slate, one of the prisoners. The other one was called Dugan."

Joe Vance put his arm around Adam's shoulders. He shook his head. "You were plumb lucky, Adam, that's all I can say . . . just plumb lucky!"

Adam picked up a plate. He wanted to change the subject. "I got a real nice dinner for you, Pa . . . and I see Uncle Seth's wagon coming." He retrieved the last dish and dusted it off.

Uncle Seth's wagon rattled up to the station. Adam's father strode over to greet him. Adam could hear them talking about the prisoners as he poured the coffee. The two walked over to the campfire, and Adam handed them their coffee.

Uncle Seth watched Adam cut a juicy slice from the roasted pig. "Adam, you're amazin'! Just amazin'! When did you have time to bag yourself a javelina with those two pesterin' no-accounts?"

Adam dropped a slice of meat onto his uncle's plate. "Oh, I shot it early this mornin' before those men got here."

"Your daddy says you stalled them off. How'd you do it?"

While his uncle and his father ate, Adam told them everything that had happened. When he came to the part where Dugan and Slate ate the rattlesnake meat, the two men threw their heads back and laughed loudly.

Uncle Seth wiped a tear from his eye. "Now if that isn't justice for you—snakes to the sneaky!" He chuckled to himself. "Come to think of it, though, rattlesnake steaks aren't bad at all. I ate some once . . . tastes a little like chicken."

Adam offered his father more meat. Joe Vance shook his head and stood up. He smiled at Adam. "Haven't room for another bite, Son. That's the best meal yet. Couldn't have done better myself!" He looked at his brother. "Brought along some tools to start clear-

72

in' brush for the new station, but these visitors sort of change our plans. You'd better high-tail it back to Rio Verde, Seth, and let the sheriff know about this."

Uncle Seth nodded. "Soon as Adam waters my horses."

Adam found his father and Uncle Seth leaning against the wagons when he brought the horses back.

Joe Vance straightened up from helping his brother hitch his team. "I hate to leave Adam here by himself tonight. Those men might come back."

Uncle Seth climbed into the wagon bed and dragged the mail sack to the side. "Not a chance of that, Joe. If those no-accounts were smart enough to get out of the hoosegow, they're smart enough to know we'd put the sheriff on their trail the minute we got back. They're probably runnin' for the border right now!"

Joe Vance shook his head. "I don't think so. Their dust would give them away." He waved his arm. "They could be waitin' right over yonder in that arroyo."

Adam's uncle put his hands on his hips. "Look, Joe, it takes me three hours to get back to Rio Verde with this wagon—less than that for Sheriff Bradly to get back here. You *know* those two aren't fixin' to sit in that arroyo waitin' for the sheriff. They're makin' tracks right now . . . probably walkin' their ponies where the sand won't make dust." Uncle Seth turned toward his wagon. "Bradly will be here before dark, and Adam's safe until then. Once the sheriff's nose is on their trail, those two are good as treed right now!"

"I hope you're right, Seth." Adam's father took the

mailbag and heaved it into his wagon.

"Sure I'm right!" Uncle Seth climbed into the wagon seat and picked up the reins. He smiled down at Adam. "Of course, if they tasted that roast javelina, they might be back to tuck the cook under their arm instead of the supplies." He waved and wheeled his wagon around toward Rio Verde.

With his team hitched, Joe Vance turned his wagon toward Ryansville, then reined the horses to a stop and jumped down. He walked back to Adam. "Go get the gun and call Reba. I'm takin' you back home with me."

Adam looked at his father in disbelief.

"Go on, now, I can't wait all day!"

Adam spread his hands. "But Pa! We can't leave all the supplies and the chickens! The coyotes would get them for *sure*!"

"And I can't leave you out here with those desperados loose!"

"Oh, Pa! You just heard what Uncle Seth said, didn't you? Those men won't be back. And if they *did* come, Sheriff Bradly would be here waitin' for them. He'll be here by dark. There won't be a thing for you to worry about."

Adam's father rubbed his chin. "If I was plumb sure he'd be here—"

Adam hurried to reassure his father. "Of course, he'll be, Pa. I'll be perfectly safe."

Joe Vance looked closely into the earnest upturned face. At last he grinned and tousled his son's dark hair with a big hand. "All right, you can stay tonight. But

74

mind, I'm gettin' someone older to take over this station."

Adam looked at his father with hurt surprise. "Why, wasn't I doin' all right?"

"You're doin' fine, Son, just fine!"

"Then why do you want to get someone else?"

Joe Vance looked across the brushland, and Adam could see those face muscles working again. "Things are too tough out here. It takes a man to handle this job."

"But Pa, I'm getting bigger, I *know* I am." Adam stretched himself up tall. "See? I'll bet I've grown an inch since I came out here."

Adam's father smiled and put his hands on Adam's shoulders. "I reckon you have, but inches don't make a man. It isn't right for me to expect a thirteen-year-old to outsmart a couple of jailbreakers, or tangle with rattlers and pesky coyotes."

Adam turned his head and winked back tears of disappointment. "If you get someone else, you'll have to pay them a lot of money to stay out here, and you won't make any money on the mail contract."

"Maybe so, but there's some things more important than money." Joe Vance gave Adam's shoulder a squeeze, then turned and walked toward the wagon.

Adam ran beside his father. "Look, Pa, I took care of the coyotes and those men. When we clear a new place for the station, there won't be any rattlesnakes to worry about."

Joe Vance nodded as he climbed into the wagon. "Maybe so, but I'm still lookin' for a man to stay out here." He glanced under the wagon seat. "Oh, nearly forgot. Here's your boots." He reached in, drew out a sturdy pair of brown boots, and handed them to Adam. "Take care, now, Son." He lowered himself into the wagon seat, slapped the reins, and waved to Adam. The wagon rolled away.

The diminishing cloud of dust blurred crazily through the angry tears that filled Adam's eyes. He *knew* he was older now than when he first arrived at the mail station. Was it only three days ago? It seemed a lot longer. Why couldn't his father see that a boy grew up fast when he had to! Adam kicked viciously at a withered mallow by the fence opening. The flat dry seeds sprayed into the air and fell into the powdered caliche, leaving small round dents where they landed. All right, *let* his father try and find someone older. Just let him try! Probably by now everyone in Ryansville knew about the rattlesnakes. His father would have a hard time finding anybody willing to stay in the run. Adam padded through the soft dust that oozed up hot between his toes. He stopped at the tent and threw the boots angrily under his cot. He didn't need them! Why was his father always treating him like a child!

He cut himself a large slice from the roasted javelina, sprawled in the shade of the tent, and tore at the tender meat with his teeth. He licked his greasy fingers and went back to the campfire for more. Reba trotted at his heels, whining for tidbits. He loosened a leg bone from the carcass on the spit and threw it at her. The meat was still hot, and Adam laughed rudely at Reba's startled shake when she seized it, then let go quickly.

Sniffing it cautiously, she pawed at the bone, as though expecting it to be cooler on the other side. With quick jerks, she dragged it into the shade behind the water barrel and sank down to gnaw.

Adam scuffed to the water barrel and drank noisily from the dipper. He wiped his mouth on his shirt sleeve and stretched out in the shade of the tent again. He put his hands under the back of his head and gazed out over the brush fence at the tops of the cholla, mesquite, and paloverdes that wavered in the heat waves rising from the hot ground. His eyes rested on the green pads of the tall prickly pear next to the cholla. Dusty purple fruit grew here and there from the flat joints.

Adam rose and went into the tent, loaded the Winchester, and came out again. He sat in the shade and aimed at a cactus pad. The gun kicked as it fired, and Adam rubbed his shoulder. The next shot sent the green pad spinning in the air. Adam whooped exultantly and aimed at another one. The cactus stem quivered. He could see the dark hole where the bullet went through. He'd outline a circle of bullet holes. Carefully, he aimed and watched with a wide grin as the holes made a crescent in the broad green pad. At the last shot, the cactus pad tore loose and hung dangling by a single fiber. One more blast, and the pad went spinning away like the other.

Adam rolled over on his back and kicked his feet in the air. Why not try aiming the gun with his feet? He lay on his back, pulled his knees up, and rested the gun barrel on his dusty bare toes. It was hard to pull the

77

trigger in such a cramped position. The gun's kick rolled him over on his side, and he laughed. The bullet missed its target. He tried it several more times, but his legs grew tired in that cramped position, and he laid the gun down.

Adam wiped the sweat from his forehead with the tail of his faded blue shirt. He looked at it critically. It was getting stiff with dirt and sweat. Juanita wouldn't be sending him clean clothes until next week. Maybe he should wash the shirt, but he couldn't spare much water from the barrel. The tank! Why hadn't he thought of it before? He'd go over to the tank, wash his shirt, and take a swim while he was at it.

Jumping up, Adam put the gun inside the tent. With Reba at his heels, he loped down the hot dusty path to the tank. The mud at the edge was sticky and cool. It sucked at his hot feet when he crossed it. Adam pulled his shirt off and waded into the pond. The sun felt warm on his thin white shoulders. Slowly, he crouched in the water and giggled at the tickling sensation of the water that soaked quickly through his jeans and rose upward along his thighs. He swashed the shirt up and down, watching the dusty blue turn to dark blue as the water soaked into it. He swished the shirt around in a circle, lost his balance, and sat down laughing. He looked at his muddy knees rising above the water. Now he'd have to wash his jeans, too.

Getting to his feet, Adam wrung the shirt out and waded ashore. He shook it vigorously and draped it over a sage bush. Water dripped from the dangling sleeves and made damp yellow spots on the ground. He stepped

78

out of his trousers and walked back into the tank again, swinging them around his head as he went. He dunked the pants and watched the legs billow with air as he tried to force them under. They took longer to wash. How good it felt to be free of clothes! He splashed to shore and hung the pants over another bush. Now for a swim!

Whooping at Reba, who barked beside him, Adam ran out into the tank, sending great sparkling fans of spray ahead of him. He waded to his thighs, then fell laughing again into the cloudy yellow water. He rolled and splashed and dog-paddled, his hands scooping up gobs of slippery mud where they touched the bottom. He threw the mud at Reba, who lay panting on the shore. He rolled over on his back, spit mouthfuls of water into the air, and watched the brilliant drops splash back around his pale, moist stomach. Leaning his head back, he let his hair float around his head.

High above in the brilliant blue sky, he could see flat little clouds moving northward. They looked like islands in a vast blue sea. He imagined he was an eagle soaring above these little islands. How far away they were! How high up he was! Adam shivered at this new sensation. Then his gaze wandered down to the edge of the sky. A thin column of white smoke was pulling upward. Adam raised his head. His wet hair streamed water down his neck. In alarm, he splashed to his feet. The smoke was coming from the mail station!

Adam stumbled out of the tank and ran up the path toward the camp. There wasn't time for clothes!

His wet shiny body dried quickly in the heat, and the sun burned his shoulders. He panted into the station. A thick column of smoke rose from the campfire. The roast javelina! He had neglected to remove it from the supports, and it had fallen into the fire. The fat spattered and hissed and sent out bright streaks of flame as it caught fire. Adam seized a piece of mesquite and pulled the smoking carcass from the coals. He had planned to have the rest of the roast pig for dinner tomorrow. Now it was ruined. He coughed and waved the smoke away with his hand. One of the hens squawked and waddled hurriedly out of the shade of the brush fence near the campfire. Adam glanced up. A thin curl of smoke was threading through the dusty hog plum. Adam's heart thumped. A burning spatter of fat must have set the fence on fire!

He ran over, scooped up handfuls of dust, and threw them onto the smoldering tinder under the fence. The smoke was still rising. He hurried to the water barrel and brought back a dipper of the precious water. The burning twigs hissed when the water struck them. Squatting down, Adam reached in with a mesquite stick and pulled the smoldering twigs into the open. He stood up. The fence was saved.

The sun felt uncomfortably hot on his shoulders, and Adam knew he must get into his clothes. He loped back to the tank. His body felt light and free—just like an Indian brave might have felt, he thought. Leaning forward slightly, he danced a few steps in the damp mud. Then, putting his hand to his mouth, he yodeled a wild Indian war whoop and splashed back into the tank to cool his shoulders. The water felt cold this time, and he winced. He waded out of the pond again, walked to the sage bushes, shook out his partly dried clothes, and put them on. The back of his shirt was dry and rough against his sunburned shoulders, but the sleeves were still damp and soft. He combed his fingers through his dripping hair, and with his damp unbuttoned shirt flapping in the warm wind, he headed back for camp.

Adam found himself suddenly very sleepy. He pulled the cot out of the tent, placed it in the lengthening shade on the east side, and stretched out on the rumpled quilt. Reba crawled underneath the cot and flopped down with grunts and sighs. The wind blowing through his damp clothes made Adam feel cool. He drew a deep breath and closed his eyes.

It was Reba who awakened him with a low growl, throaty and menacing. Adam sat up and rubbed his eyes. The sun had disappeared behind the western hills, and the nighthawks wheeled in the pale golden afterglow, high over the tank. Reba growled again, and Adam listened intently. Above the nighthawks' cries, he could hear the jingle of bridles and squeak of saddle leather. He jumped to his feet, his heart thumping. Could Slate and Dugan be returning?

Quickly, he dragged the cot back into the tent. With shaking hands, he reached for the Winchester and loaded it. Maybe he shouldn't have wasted so many bullets that afternoon, shooting at the cactus. He hesitated for a moment. Should he go outside, or hide in the tent? Reba was barking furiously. Adam lifted the flap and called to her, but she paid no attention to him. He reached out, grabbed her by the scruff of the neck, and pulled her back into the tent beside him. "Now, hush up, Reba!" he commanded.

Adam peered cautiously through the tent opening, his gun held ready. He heard horses' hoofs stamping outside the fence, then soft "whoas." His hands tightened on the Winchester. It was quiet for a while, then a voice called out, "Adam Vance! You in there?" It didn't sound like Slate or Dugan. Adam squinted through the tent flaps again. A tall man with a broad hat shadowing his face stood in the fence opening, his feet apart, his hands at his sides. Adam could see a heavy holster slung low on the man's hips. There were other men behind him, some still on their horses.

Adam stuck his head out of the tent, but he still held the gun. The man saw him and came forward. "Don't be afraid, Adam, I'm Sheriff Bradly. Your Uncle Seth told me about your trouble this morning." The man reached the tent and threw the flap back.

Adam felt foolish standing there with the Winchester trained on the sheriff's stomach. He lowered the gun and grinned weakly. "I thought you were Slate or Dugan coming back."

The other men had dismounted and stood behind the sheriff, smiling at each other. Sheriff Bradly turned to the men. "Now, there's a young man I could use for a deputy!"

They laughed.

The sheriff turned back to Adam. "Come outside, son, and tell me just what happened."

Adam stood the gun in the corner and joined the men. He wondered why there were so many looking for two unarmed swindlers. Some of the men stood with their arms folded across their chests, some squatted on their heels while Adam related his morning's adventure.

When he had finished, Sheriff Bradly patted Adam on the shoulder. "You're a smart young man, Adam! Under the circumstances, I couldn't have done better myself. By stallin' those two, you helped us more than you realize."

Adam looked up questioningly at the sheriff.

"We found out this mornin' they're wanted up north for robbin' a bank and killin' a man. But thanks to you, Adam, we'll have those two back in Rio Verde in no time flat. So as you won't worry none, I'll leave one of my men with you."

"Oh, you don't need to do that, Sheriff, I'll be fine."

"You sure now?"

"I'm sure, sir."

Sheriff Bradly patted Adam's arm and grinned at him. "You've got more spunk than most young'uns, I'll say that." He turned. "All right, let's go, men."

Sheriff Bradly walked toward the fence opening, and the other men followed. They mounted their horses quickly and headed in the direction Adam had pointed out to them.

Adam felt a wave of relief wash over him. He scooched down and hugged Reba. "No more Slate or Dugan to worry about! Did you hear that, Reba?" The dog wagged her white-tipped tail and licked Adam's ear with a moist pink tongue. Adam picked up a small stick and threw it to the other end of the compound. "Fetch!" he cried.

Reba bounded after the stick. She jarred the brush fence in turning, and the hens teetering on a mesquite branch squawked in protest, flapping their wings to keep their balance. With the stick in her mouth, Reba trotted back to Adam. He threw it again and again, until Reba grew tired and wandered off to investigate a lizard making its way through the fence.

The first coyote wail floated through the dusk. Adam threw more wood on the fire. Funny, but that cry didn't bother him any more. He smiled when he remembered how frightened he had been that first night. He glanced about the brush fence. There! He had forgotten to pull the brush across the opening. He padded over and dragged a mesquite branch into place.

A motion in the thick dust just outside made him stop. Two large rattlesnakes glided across the hoofprints made by the horses. He watched their graceful bodies flow forward with heads held slightly above their diamond backs. They were moving toward the tank. He watched them until they disappeared in the dusk. He pulled more brush across the opening. That was strange.

Those rattlers hadn't frightened him either. He adjusted the last branch. It would be a lot easier if he had a real gate to close at night. Maybe when they moved to the new mail station his father could build him one.

Suddenly he remembered his father's last words that afternoon—"I'm goin' to look for a man to stay out here." Disappointment welled up in him. Just when he was getting used to coyotes, and he wasn't afraid of rattlers any more. Just when there weren't any more criminals to worry about, he would have to leave. He'd *never* get to prove to his father that he wasn't a boy any more!

Adam sank down by the fire and hugged his knees. A warm breeze smelling of dusty sage and creosote bushes rumpled his hair. He looked up at the black bowl of stars glittering above him. He liked it here. Why must he leave? Reba came over and lay down at his feet, her nose towards the crackling fire. The coyotes were calling back and forth. Adam watched Reba's ears move with each wail. He grinned. "Why, *you're* getting used to the coyotes, too, aren't you, Reba!" He patted her black flank shining in the firelight, and she sighed contentedly. Even Reba liked it here. Oh well, he wouldn't think about leaving—it would only make him feel sad.

With the fire dying down, Adam yawned loudly. He had had a busy day; it was time to turn in. He banked the glowing coals with the ashes and shuffled into the dark tent. The cot creaked as Reba jumped up and stretched out beside him. "Move over, you old hound, you're crowding me," Adam muttered sleepily, but he really didn't mind. He liked Reba's warm body close beside him.

It was near midnight when Reba's rumbling growl awakened Adam. She still lay at his side, but her head was up and her body tense against his. Adam rose on his elbows and listened. Reba growled again. "Oh hush, Reba!" he whispered.

At first he could hear only the crickets chirping. Then he heard a soft scratching sound like someone dragging branches across the ground. Reba jumped off the cot and stuck her head through the tent opening. Adam climbed quickly out of bed and, kneeling beside the dog, held her back. She growled again. "Will you hush, Reba?" he repeated.

Slowly he lifted the tent flap and looked out. It was dark in the tent, but outside in the glow of the stars, he could make out the form of the brush fence. His gaze traveled around its top to the opening he had filled with brush that evening. He drew in his breath. The palms of his hands felt sweaty. Someone was quietly pulling the mesquite branches out one by one.

Suddenly the dark figure of a man slid silently into the compound. The man moved forward like a cougar, stopped to listen, then beckoned toward the opening. Another figure stole in beside him. This one was short and fat, and the top of his head glistened in the starlight. It was Slate and Dugan!

6

ADAM's first impulse was to grab the Winchester and shoot at the men's feet. It would scare them away, certainly, but not for long. Slate and Dugan wanted the gun and supplies; he was sure of it now. They would be back. They were clever and dangerous men. Adam remembered how he had scoffed at his father's concern that afternoon. Sheriff Bradly would be here, Adam had assured his father. Where *was* Sheriff Bradly now? He wished he had accepted the sheriff's offer and let one of the men from the posse stay at the mail station with him. How could these two have eluded the posse?

Adam's mouth and throat felt suddenly dry. He swallowed. The back of his neck prickled and made him shiver. He didn't feel a bit grown up. He wished he could run away. Why hadn't he listened to his father and gone back to town with him? Adam remembered the trick he had played on Slate that afternoon to keep him from going into the tent. He wondered if they had tied the horses to the same mesquite tree. He listened intently. Yes, he could hear a snort and a shuffle of hoofs near the fence opening. But his trick wouldn't work now. He was inside the tent, and the desperados were creeping slowly toward it.

Reba growled, and the men stopped. Adam wondered what he should do. He knew they needed their horses to travel. If there was some way he could untie the ponies, Slate and Dugan would have to go after them on foot. And with the rattlesnakes all around the station at night, the two weren't likely to come back before morning. Sheriff Bradly would surely catch them by then. If he could get outside without Dugan or Slate seeing him, he might untie the horses and frighten them away. But he couldn't slap the horses or shout at them —the men would hear him. What could he use? He remembered the rattlesnake buttons he had placed under his bedding. Horses would shy and run if they heard a rattlesnake sing. Adam crept back to the bed and felt under the cot pad. Yes, there they were. He slipped the two biggest strings of rattles into his pants pocket and tiptoed back to Reba. "Now stay!" he ordered. Reba growled at the approaching men.

Adam slipped softly to the back of the dark tent and felt along the canvas wall till he touched the cold metal barrel of the Winchester. It was still loaded from the evening before. He dared not leave it. He knelt on the ground and forced the back of the tent up. It was staked down tightly, and he had difficulty squeezing under it. The gun barrel struck a tent stake and clanked loudly. Flat on his stomach, Adam held his breath. He was halfway out of the tent. Had the men heard? Reba's growls were growing louder. She would be barking soon. He pulled himself out from under the tent and, sliding the gun along the ground ahead of him, rose to his hands and knees. Along the rear of the tent he crawled to the right corner and peeked around.

Slate and Dugan were nearing the front of the tent. He could see something in Slate's hands. It looked like a thick stick of firewood. Adam swallowed again. He knew they meant to harm him. It was a good thing for him he had crawled out of the tent, but what about Reba? Would they hurt her? Adam hesitated. Maybe he should shoot now. He wouldn't be trapped in the tent; he could run away if he had to. But if he fired, the gun would give him away, and the men could reach the horses before he had a chance to untie them. Reba was smart enough not to let them hit her. She could keep them busy long enough for him to run to the horses. Barking filled the tent, and Adam could hear Slate cursing softly. With the gun under his arm, Adam got to his feet and crept around the tent to the side nearest the fence opening.

Reba yelped suddenly as though she had been kicked. He heard her whimper and scramble out from under the tent. Her slick body trembled against his legs. Adam reached down and, holding her tightly, put his mouth against her ear. "You're all right now, Reba, so hush up, you hear?" he whispered tensely. Reba was silent.

Adam peered cautiously around the front corner of the tent. Slate and Dugan were creeping inside. He heard the stick hit the cot heavily several times. Adam was glad he wasn't in bed. Quickly, he scampered across the compound and out through the opening that Slate had made in the fence. Reba followed at his heels. Adam stopped in the thick dust outside.

The two ponies tied to the mesquite tree loomed to his left. He approached them quietly. One turned its head and nickered at him. He felt along their sweaty sides. They had been running. It was about time they were free. Adam patted their wet necks. He leaned the Winchester against the mesquite tree and fumbled in the dark with the tight knots. The horses pulled at the reins impatiently.

"Just a minute, you two," Adam whispered. At last the knots loosened and he dropped the reins to the ground. Adam reached into his pocket and pulled the rattlesnake tails out. He held them in front of the horses and shook the buttons vigorously. The ponies snorted and backed off. One neighed loudly and, wheeling around, galloped off into the night. The other one trotted after him.

Adam picked up the gun and crept along the fence away from the opening. He could hear Slate and Dugan arguing loudly. They came out of the tent.

Dugan sounded angry. "I tell you I *did* hear those horses running!"

Slate sounded even angrier. "You're hearin' things! They neighed, sure, but I've got 'em tied out there so they'd *never* get away. Come on, no use looking for the gun any longer."

Dugan's voice was bitter. "That smart brat probably left with his daddy this afternoon and took the gun with him."

"What about that noisy cur?" Slate asked.

"Reckon they left *him* to watch the place."

Slate snickered. "Some watchdog!" He started for the fence opening.

Dugan paused by the tent. "Just a minute, Slate, we might as well help ourselves to a little coffee and bacon. Can't travel on an empty stomach."

Slate sounded impatient. "How you goin' to find things in the dark? Look, Dugan, we gave that posse the slip once. Don't push our luck."

Dugan was lifting the tent flap. "With my keen sense of smell, I'll locate the food right away."

"Your keen sense of smell! That's what fouled us up this mornin'! If you hadn't stood around sniffing that roast pig, we coulda been in Mexico by now with a Winchester and a sack of grub, too."

"Now don't be impatient, Slate. Here, grab this flour sack. I'll take the coffeepot."

Slate strode back and grabbed the sack out of Dugan's hand. "Next time I'll pick me a skinny partner!"

Dugan stopped. "I resent that, Slate! You couldn't get anywhere without my brains!"

Slate laughed shortly. "That stomach of yours cancels out your brains!"

While Dugan and Slate walked toward the fence opening, Adam, bent low, peered intently at the dark ground and crept along the brush fence around the corner. He paused. He mustn't go too far. It was dangerous to walk outside the camp at night with the rattlesnakes all around. He wished he had put on his boots.

Dugan was first to discover that the horses were gone. His voice rose in a frenzied shout. "See? See? What did I tell you, Slate? I *knew* I heard those horses running!"

Slate was cursing loudly. "I knotted them reins so they *couldn't* pull loose! *Somebody* untied them! I'll bet that brat is still around here!"

Adam squeezed tight against the fence, his heart pounding.

Dugan scoffed. "That's ridiculous! Where could he hide?"

Slate's voice sounded ominous. "He's out here *somewhere,* and he's got that gun with him. Come on! You go around the fence that way, I'll go this way. We'll find him!"

Adam moved farther along the brush fence, Reba close beside him.

"See here, Slate. Don't waste time, nobody's around here. Those reins *pulled* loose . . . your carelessness as usual!"

Slate turned on Dugan. "Careless, am I? Who was careless this mornin'? Who let a brat talk him into waitin' for dinner?"

"Now just a minute! We had to have grub, didn't we?"

The men were arguing violently when Adam heard a horse whinny. Slate and Dugan heard it, too. They stopped talking.

In the sudden silence, Adam was sure they could

hear his heart beating. Why hadn't the ponies gone farther away? Now Slate and Dugan would catch them and be back to the mail station to find him! His plan wasn't working out at all.

Dugan spoke first. His voice was low and excited. "By George, I think I see one! Yes, there it is, over to the right . . . And we're in luck! The other pony's with it!"

Adam could hear the men running.

Slate spoke sharply. "Get out of my way, Dugan!"

"Quit shovin'! Can't you see that rattler just ahead?"

"Well, go around him."

"Can't, there's one on either side."

Adam heard the ponies snort and trot toward the tank.

"Let me by, will you? I got to catch those ponies."

Dugan sounded breathless. "Go ahead! Go right ahead and step on those rattlers! I'm watching my step. There's another one!"

The cursing voices of the men and the retreating hoofbeats of the ponies grew fainter and fainter. Reba sat down on Adam's feet, and he bent to stroke her. "Well, Reba," he sighed softly, "Slate and Dugan have a long run ahead of them. Those ponies aren't fixin' to be caught!"

Adam slipped back to the fence opening, still watching the ground. He put his hands in his pockets, felt the rattlesnake tails, and drew one out. He tossed it up and down in his hand smiling to himself. Pretty clever trick of his—frightening the horses that way. The buttons rattled faintly as he tossed them. He missed the catch, and a tail fell into the dust. He leaned over and felt about in the dark. That was his biggest rattle . . . he didn't want to lose it. Funny, he could still hear those buttons. It sounded over by the mesquite tree. Yes, he could see them gleaming dully in the starlight.

Adam took a step toward the tree and stopped. The buttons were moving back and forth with the dark coils of a snake's body attached to them. He lifted the Winchester to his shoulder and took aim, then he lowered the gun. No, he mustn't shoot. The noise would bring Slate and Dugan back for sure. He tucked the gun under his arm and laughed to himself. Just let Slate try tying the horses to that mesquite tree now. Old Mr. Rattlesnake could stay right there! He'd make a fine guard for the mail station!

Inside the compound Adam laid the gun down and pulled the brush into place. He picked the Winchester up and stumbled to the tent. It still wasn't safe to go to sleep. He had better keep watch for a while. Next time Slate and Dugan came, he would shoot near their feet until his ammunition ran out. He wished he hadn't wasted so many bullets on the cactus pads.

Adam fastened the tent curtains back and pulled the cot over to where he could watch the entrance. He sat down and looked up at the sky. The stars glittered like reflected chips of torchlight on a midnight pond. The crickets' high chirping pulsed rhythmically through the brush fence. A light cool breeze, fragrant with sage, flapped the tent top up and down. Adam leaned back on the bed. It was wonderful out here when the nights were like this.

All at once Adam felt like crying. He didn't know why. He'd outsmarted Slate and Dugan again, hadn't he? His father would be pleased with that. He'd been brave as a man ought to be. Yet now he didn't want to be brave any more. He wished he were little again. He wanted to run and climb into his father's arms where he was safe, where nothing could happen to him.

Adam put his arms up over his face. Hot tears trickled toward his ears. He rolled over and wiped his face on the quilt. This was ridiculous! He wasn't little any more. He was thirteen, and on his own. He had to be brave even though it was scary sometimes. Tomorrow, when he told his father about the outlaws' return, he would—Adam sat up. Why, he didn't *dare* tell his father about tonight. His father would be angry for having listened to him. His father would say, "I told you so," and pack Adam off home with the first mail bags. There would be no more hunts in the brushland; no more swims in the tank; no more quiet moments like this to look at the stars. No, he mustn't tell him.

The swift shadowy form of an owl stopped in mid-air, hovered for a second near the cholla, then dropped out of sight. It rose a moment later with a small dark animal struggling in its claws. Silently, it disappeared over the tent. Why couldn't Sheriff Bradly catch Slate and Dugan like that? Leaning forward, Adam looked out at an imaginary flying man. "By George, Reba," he mimicked, "There goes Sheriff Bradly. Now he's hovering . . . now down . . . he's up again . . . he's got one! No, he's got two of them, by George!" Adam leaned back and giggled. How funny Dugan would look sailing through the air in Sheriff Bradly's clutches!

The laugh faded away. Adam sat up again. What if Sheriff Bradly and his men missed Dugan and Slate completely? What if the desperados came back again? He mustn't go to sleep. Adam peered intently at the brush fence. Nothing yet. He hoped the rattlesnake was still out there at the foot of the mesquite. Funny, he never thought he'd be glad to live in a rattlesnake run!

A lone coyote wail rippled across the night. It seemed almost human. The answering "yip, yip, yip, ow-o-o," sent sound across sound. He wondered where the coyotes were tonight . . . not around the mail station, certainly. Were they following Slate and Dugan?

A shot echoed through the brushland. Then another . . . and another. Adam leaned forward. Sheriff Bradly must have found the criminals! Adam hoped they had given up quietly. Though he disliked Slate and Dugan, he didn't like to think of them being shot. He listened for more gunfire, but it had ceased. Now he could go back to sleep! Adam stretched out under the quilt and closed his eyes.

The eastern sky was reddening when Adam awoke. He couldn't have been asleep very long, he thought. Reba was outside barking at something. Adam rolled over on his stomach and raised himself on his elbows. He looked across the fence at a drifting cloud of dust.

96

There was the clop, clop of a horse coming toward the mail station. Adam got to his knees and leaned over for the Winchester propped against the supplies. He laid the gun beside him under the quilt. There were cries of "whoa," and Sheriff Bradly called over the fence. "You all right, Adam?"

Adam jumped out of the cot and ran toward the brush that filled the fence opening. "Sure, Sheriff, I'm fine." He pulled hastily at the mesquite branches.

Sheriff Bradly strode into camp. "Got a little worried about you when I found these." He held out the coffeepot and a sack with coffee beans dripping from a hole.

Adam took them. "Thanks. Did you find them on Dugan?"

"No, it's a funny thing. The pot was lyin' under a prickly pear bush out yonder with a rattler curled up inside it. The sack was farther on a piece."

Adam grinned. "Guess Dugan must have dropped them last night."

"Then they did come back here! Thought for sure they wouldn't. About what time was it?"

Adam told Sheriff Bradly everything that had happened.

The sheriff smiled and shook his head. "You're a mighty brave young man to have hung onto that gun. Those two *hombres* would have done anything to get hold of it."

"Where'd you catch them, Sheriff?"

"Well, Adam, *we* didn't exactly catch them.

Adam looked alarmed. "What do you mean?"

The sheriff shifted his feet. "You see, we found their ponies halfway back to Rio Verde, still saddled and draggin' their reins, but no hide nor hair of Dugan and Slate."

Adam's face fell.

Sheriff Bradly grinned at the crestfallen boy. "So we circled back this way. Can't guess where we found those two *hombres*!"

"Where?" Adam asked with relief in his voice.

"Sittin' in a mesquite tree having a cussfight, with a herd of javelinas millin' around underneath clickin' their teeth at 'em!"

Adam heaved a big sigh. "Then you didn't shoot Dugan or Slate? I was afraid you had to, when I heard those shots."

"No, Adam, we fired those shots to scare away the javelinas." Sheriff Bradly smiled. "Dugan and Slate seemed right glad to see us. Went back meek as rabbits. Kept mumblin' something about rattlers, rattlers everywhere."

Relief overwhelmed Adam. He began to laugh. He couldn't stop. Sheriff Bradly looked at Adam, now doubled over with laughter, and chuckled.

Adam finally got hold of himself and wiped the tears from his eyes. He glanced at the pot still in his hand. "Let me fix you some coffee, Sheriff. I'll have the fire ready and beans ground in no time."

"Thanks, Adam. That's real thoughtful of you, but I've got to get back to Rio Verde. Just wanted to make

99

sure you were all right." Sheriff Bradly turned and walked toward the fence opening. He waved to Adam. "Take care, now." He mounted his pony and headed back across the brushland.

Adam turned and capered a few steps on the hard caliche. "Oh, Reba! Can't you just see Slate and Dugan havin' a cussfight in that mesquite tree? Those two would argue anywhere. I'll bet they're arguin' in the hoosegow right now!"

Adam walked over to the campfire, brushed the ashes back from the coals, and had a blaze crackling in a few minutes. He skirted the fence and found three eggs in the brush. They were soon sizzling in the skillet. He was hungry this morning.

With his breakfast over, Adam wondered what he could have for his father's dinner. He'd been so busy with Slate and Dugan, he'd forgotten all about the noon meal. He wished he hadn't been so careless and let the roast pig burn yesterday. There had been plenty of meat for another meal. Now the charred carcass lay in the dust near the end of the compound where Reba had dragged it. Big red ants scurried over it, cleaning the bones. He must take it out of the station before his father arrived. Picking up the shovel, he carefully lifted the carcass and walked rapidly with it out through the fence opening and around to the side. Red ants dropped to the ground in bunches, and Adam in his bare feet had to watch that he didn't step on them. With a big heave, he threw the bones out among the cactus.

Back in the station, he cleaned the skillet, watered

and fed the chickens, and pushed the cot back into place in the tent. He smoothed out the quilts and stood the gun in the corner. There, his chores were done. He came out of the tent and squinted at the sun. It was too late in the morning for hunting. Might be a few quail near the tank, but he didn't want to cook any more quail. The tank! Surely there must be *some* fish in it! He went back into the tent and lifted out his fishing pole, which stood beside the Winchester. It was a long pole, thin and supple, made out of willow. He had caught lots of perch and bass with this pole when he fished back home in Ryan Creek. Adam stuffed an empty flour sack into his back pocket, went outside, and started down the path toward the tank. Reba ran ahead of him.

He stopped in the hot path. Bait! He'd need bait if he planned to fish. Perch liked grasshoppers . . . there must be some around here. He searched the dusty grass and *perezia* along the pathway. Ah, there was one! Quickly Adam laid his pole down, cupped his right hand, and clapped it over the hopper. He could feel the sting of its rough legs snap upward against his fingers. Reaching in with his other hand, he carefully picked it up by the joints of its back legs. He pulled the flour sack out of his pocket and stuffed the struggling hopper far back into a corner of the sack. He rubbed the palms of his hand against his jeans to remove the brown juice the grasshopper had sprayed on him. He looked about for more insects. He was in luck. There were lots of grass-hoppers about this morning.

At last, one corner of the flour sack snapped and

rustled with hoppers. Adam picked up his pole and trudged on to the tank. He paused at its muddy edge. He couldn't fish here, it was too shallow. Maybe across the pond he could find a deeper spot. The brush grew thick and close to the limestone ledge over there, but he was sure he could get through. He walked quickly around the pond.

With his pole held high over his head, Adam pushed through the scrub cedar, mesquite, and hog plum. Once, the flour sack caught on a sharp thorn, and he nearly lost the grasshoppers. But he finally broke through to the narrow limestone ledge whose rough surface, hot against the soles of his feet, dropped abruptly to the water three feet below.

Adam leaned over and peered into the water. Near the surface, tiny specks of sediment glinted in the sunlight, but it was dark and murky down deep. A mesquite leaf suspended upright just below the surface of the water turned slowly. The spring that fed the tank must be directly underneath, he thought. He searched the depths for movements of fish. A slender shadow darted away from the ledge . . . it must be a perch. Hurriedly, he hooked a grasshopper onto his line, dropped the bait into the water, and watched the ripples travel out from the red cork bobber. Each ripple struck the limestone bank under him with a soft slap, slap.

He sat down on the warm rock. The smell of cedar needles, warm and pungent, drifted across the air. Adam's eyes traveled from the water to the quivering wings of an iridescent red "snake doctor" hovering directly in front of him. He watched it dart in sweeping arcs over the tank. It would hover for an instant just above the surface, dip its tail into the water, and send tiny radiant ripples traveling toward shore.

Swinging his legs, Adam watched their reflection move back and forth in the water. He did like to fish, even better than he liked to hunt . . . better than anything else he could think of. A slender blue mosquito hawk, fragile and lovely, landed lightly on the edge of the limestone and folded narrow shimmering wings over its back. Strange, he thought, such a beautiful creature here in the wild dry brushland. But then, wherever you found water you always found mosquito hawks. Out of the corner of his eye, Adam caught the agitated bobbing of the cork. He gave a quick upward yank to set the hook, then jerked his line from the water. A wriggling perch arced toward him, its yellow belly flashing in the sun. Adam caught the line a short distance above the fish and dropped the pole. He waited till the perch had quieted for a moment, then carefully brought his other hand downward from the fish's head. Seizing it so the sharp back fins lay flat against its back, he removed the hook and smiled with satisfaction at the gasping fish slightly larger than his hand. He stuffed the perch into the flour sack and pulled out another grasshopper. If he could catch about a dozen of these, he'd have a fine dinner.

He dropped his line farther out this time. The bobber had hardly hit the water when it ducked out of sight. He pulled out another perch. He glanced over at

Reba stretched in the shade of a scrub cedar, her eyes half open, her nose on her paws. "You better like perch, Reba, there's goin' to be plenty for dinner," he said.

An hour later, with the flour sack wet and lumpy with perch, Adam glanced up at the sun. He had eleven fish; better stop now. He'd have to hurry if he expected to have these cleaned and fried by the time his father and Uncle Seth arrived.

Back in the mail station, Adam threw more wood on the fire. He put the skillet on and fried a few slices of bacon. He rolled the cleaned fish in the top of the cornmeal sack and, holding them by the tails, dropped them into the hot skillet. They sizzled and spattered hot grease into the fire, where bright little flames flared for a moment, then sputtered out.

The smell of frying fish drifted through the fence opening when Adam's father pulled up to the mail station. Adam, busy with the fish, didn't notice the slender young man sitting on the seat beside Joe Vance.

Adam heard his father's voice boom out. "Well, here we are, Frank, and it smells like we're havin' a fish fry."

Adam looked up quickly. Who could the visitor be? he wondered. The stranger climbed out of the wagon and turned toward the camp. He was tall and in his early twenties, Adam figured. A black felt hat, new and jaunty, shaded his thin face. He wore a high collar and a dark vest under a suit coat powdered now with cal-iche. His fancy tan boots sank into the thick dust near the fence entrance as he followed Adam's father toward the campfire.

Joe Vance put his hand on the young man's shoulder. "Frank, this is my son, Adam. Adam, this is Frank Whipple."

Adam wiped his right palm on his jeans and took the lean hand extended to him. His shoulder shook with the vigorous pumping of Frank's firm grip.

"It's a real pleasure to meet you, Adam," he said.

Joe Vance smiled at his son. "Frank, here, is a nephew of Doc Anders. Came out from New York to visit his uncle." He turned to Frank. "Doc says you want to see more of the West."

"That's right, Mr. Vance." His voice was high-pitched. "This is marvelous country! Such blue sky! Such fresh air!" Frank put his hand on his chest and took a deep breath. "Ah-h-h-h!" he exhaled. He started to draw another deep breath, but a wisp of campfire smoke blew suddenly across his face, and he broke into a fit of coughing.

Joe Vance patted him on the back. "Sure do appreciate your comin' out to help. But remember, like I said, it's mighty rugged livin' in this brush country."

Frank caught his breath. "I understand your concern for me, Mr. Vance. However, you needn't worry. I've done a lot of roughing it in the Adirondacks. Camping is much the same anywhere you go."

Adam's father turned to him. "Forgot to tell you, Son. Frank, here, is takin' over the mail station."

105

7

ADAM ducked his head and busied himself with the coffeepot. Why did his father have to find someone so soon? Adam didn't want to leave the mail station now, when he'd found such a good fishing spot. Why couldn't his father have waited a few days? Adam heard Uncle Seth's wagon arrive, but he didn't look toward his uncle. He heard Frank being introduced to Uncle Seth, then the three men walking toward the fire. Adam kept his head down even when he filled the plates with fish and handed them around.

Joe Vance beckoned for Frank to join them where they squatted in the tent shade, but Frank preferred to stand. Adam poured coffee and brought it to the men.

Adam's father looked up. "I clean forgot, Adam. Under the wagon seat, there's a couple of loaves of bread Juanita baked. Might fetch them and cut us a few slices."

Adam shuffled to the wagon. Besides the loaves of bread were Frank's cot, bedroll, shiny new rifle, and a large dusty suitcase. Adam wondered if the suitcase was

106

full of clothes. If so, it was certainly more than Frank would need out here. He brought the bread back and cut thick slices.

His father helped himself. "After you've watered the horses, Son, bring Frank's things into the tent. I reckon it would be best if you stayed here with him for a few days till he gets the feel of the job."

Adam scuffed the ground. He looked at Frank, who was patting his mouth with a white handkerchief. "If you're through eatin', would you like to come see where we water the horses?"

"I most certainly would, Adam. There's no time like the present, as the saying goes, is there?" Frank put his cup and plate down and strode after the boy.

Adam reached the horses and turned to Frank. "We might as well take both teams at once, since there's two of us. I usually take one at a time. You unhitch Uncle Seth's team and I'll take care of Pa's."

"Sure thing, Adam. Many hands make light work, eh, friend?" Frank fumbled with the harnesses.

Adam started down the path. He glanced back. Frank was following, but the horses, not used to a strange person leading them, were jerking their heads up and down.

"Steady, there, steady!" Frank was gripping the reins and leaning back. When Uncle Seth's team neared the water, they broke into a trot, pulling poor Frank after them at a jogging run. "Whoa-o-o!" he panted.

Frank's boots sank into the sticky mud near the edge of the water. One mired down so deeply that he couldn't lift it out. The horses yanked him forward again and, being unable to stop, Frank was catapulted out of his boot. He stood teetering on one foot at the edge of the water. He tried hard to keep from stepping in the mud with his stockinged foot, but the team jerked their heads once more, and Frank lost his balance completely. He sat down in the yellow muck with a loud smack.

Adam wanted to laugh, but he dared not. Frank struggled to his feet muttering. He looked ruefully at the great muddy spot on his pants and at his slimy yellow sock. Adam led his own team close to Frank's. "Here, I'll take your team while you get your boot."

"Thanks, Adam." Frank handed him the reins.

The boot came out of the mud with a slow sucking sound, and Frank hobbled up the path towards camp, his muddy sock gathering a thick coating of dust. He didn't stop until he reached the wagon. He pulled his suitcase from under the seat and heaved it to the ground. He grasped his rifle, picked the suitcase up, and limped into the tent.

Adam tied Uncle Seth's team to the mesquite tree while he hitched his father's horses to the wagon. He was just finishing when the two men came over.

Uncle Seth took his team. "What happened to Frank?"

Adam grinned. "Fell down in the mud."

His father looked sharply at Adam. "Now see here, Son, I don't want any monkey business goin' on with Frank."

"I didn't do a thing, Pa, honest! One of his boots

stuck in the mud and he lost his balance, that's all!"

Uncle Seth snickered and nodded toward the tent. "Appears to me he knows as much about horses as a hog knows about Sunday."

Joe Vance frowned. "Now don't make fun of him, Seth. It may take him a little while to get used to things out here, but he'll manage. He's a smart young man."

Uncle Seth backed his horses into place. "Well, he won't have to worry about those outlaws. Forgot to tell you, Joe. Sheriff Bradly brought them in early this morning."

Adam's father looked pleased. "Sure enough?" He glanced at Adam. "When did the sheriff get here last night?"

"Right after sundown."

"How about those criminals? They come around again?"

Adam hesitated. Should he tell his father what had really happened? Sheriff Bradly had said he was a mighty brave boy. But would his father think so? Most likely his father would shake his head and say, "I shouldn't have listened to you yesterday." No, he'd better not say anything about it. Adam was suddenly aware of his father's voice.

"What, Pa?"

"I said did those jailbreakers come around again?"

Adam looked at the ground. "Not while the posse was here." He added hastily, "But I heard Sheriff Bradly's shots when he caught them."

As soon as he had answered, Adam felt squirmy inside. It had been the truth, but only part of it. He wondered if his father would notice.

But his answer seemed to satisfy Joe Vance, and he jumped into the wagon. "That's a load off my mind. With those two back where they belong, we can start clearin' brush for the new station tomorrow." He lifted Frank's bedroll and cot down to Adam. "You be helpful, Son, you hear?"

"Yes, Pa."

Joe Vance called toward the tent. "We're leavin' now, Frank, any message you want me to give Doc?"

Frank stuck his head out. "No thanks, Mr. Vance, not today."

The two men clucked to their horses and drove off in opposite directions.

Adam lifted the heavy cot in one hand and the bed roll in the other. His shoulders sagged under the weight, and he walked with short rapid steps across the hot ground to the tent.

Frank came outside.

Adam saw that Frank had changed clothes and was wearing a pair of dark narrow shoes, gray pants, and a light blue shirt stiff with starch. He had left off his coat, vest, and stiff collar, but his black hat sat jauntily on his head. He rubbed the palms of his hands together briskly.

"Well, now," he said brightly, "let's get organized." He smiled at Adam. "Great fun camping, eh, my friend? Let's take care of this cot first." He held back the tent flap. "You can put it right in there, Adam. Better set it up against the back wall."

110

Adam picked the bedding up again and heaved it into the tent. It was stuffy and hot working in the tent, but Adam soon had the cot assembled and the bedding smoothed out upon it. He stepped from the tent and wiped his sweaty forehead on his shirt sleeve.

Frank was busily scraping at the dried caliche on his gaily stitched boots. Adam collected the dirty dishes and walked to the campfire.

Frank looked over at him. "Haven't you anything to sit on around here besides the cots?" he asked.

"The ground," Adam answered shortly.

"That seems a little primitive in this day and age of camp stools." Frank gazed about the camp. "Yes, to get this station running in tip-top order, we'll need a few more things . . . a canvas shelter, some camp stools, a table. . . ." He walked over to where Adam squatted by the fire, scouring the skillet out with ashes. "Why on earth are you doing it *that* way? Haven't you any soap and water?"

"Can't waste it." Adam nodded toward the water barrel. "That's all the water we've got, and we need it for cookin' and drinkin'."

"Looks to me like you're making more work for yourself than is necessary."

Adam glanced up, his face red with the heat of the fire and his anger rising. "There's nothin' wrong with the way I'm doin' things! I've managed all right so far!"

"Of course you have, Adam," Frank hastened to assure him. "But you're doing it the hard way." Frank rubbed his boots with a soft cloth, then walked to the end of the compound and hung them upside down on a mesquite branch. He came back. "I'd better make a list of the things we need." He walked into the tent.

Adam followed him with the clean dishes, carefully stacking them on top of the supplies. Frank sat down on his cot, pulled a pad and pencil from his pocket, and began writing busily. It was too hot in the tent for Adam. He dragged his cot outside into the east shade. With a big sigh, he tumbled onto the quilt.

Staying in the mail station wasn't a bit of fun any more. Just as well he was going home with his father in a day or two. It wouldn't be camping with stools and tables and shelters cluttering up the place. Adam rolled over on his back and put his arms up over his eyes. Heat waves rose from the ground and blew across his face. The hot dry air made his eyes sting, his skin draw tight over his cheekbones, and his lips feel as if they were cracking. He wished he were swimming right now. He would dive like a fish to the shady depths of the spring that fed the tank. There he would let the fresh cold water flow from its secret cave in the limestone ledge and fan over his face. When its chill penetrated to his bones, he would drift upward and float suspended near the surface, where the specks of sediment glinted in the sunlight. He would let the boil of the spring water turn him slowly as it did the mesquite leaf.

Someone shook his shoulder briskly, and Adam lifted his arms from his eyes. Frank stood by his cot smiling down at him. "Let's be up and at it, Adam. We can save the snoozing for night time."

Adam glanced about. It was still early afternoon. "It's too hot to do anything yet," he mumbled.

"Now, now, my friend, if we want an efficient mail station we'll have to work at it. Mustn't be lazy."

Adam rubbed his eyes and sat up. "I'm not lazy, just tired. I didn't get much sleep last night."

"What kept you awake?"

Adam remembered his harrowing night with Slate and Dugan. He'd like to tell Frank all about it. But if he did, Frank might tell Adam's father, who would surely be angry because Adam had kept it from him. "Oh, just—some things."

Frank patted Adam on the shoulder. "You can go to bed early tonight. Right now let's make a list of our duties around here." Frank pulled the pad and pencil out again and sat down beside Adam. "You see, Adam, organizing everything on paper this way saves a lot of time. Now, what things need to be done in order, starting with the morning?"

Adam scratched his head. "Guess gettin' up is first. After that I do whatever job seems most important."

Frank sighed patiently. "That's your whole trouble, Adam, no set plan. Make yourself a schedule and stick to it. Then your day will run like clockwork."

"But supposin' things don't work out like you want."

"They'll work out if you plan ahead."

"But supposin'—"

"Stop supposing and tell me what needs to be done now!" Frank was curt.

Adam named over the activities, and Frank jotted

113

them down in neat order.

"We'll need more wood for the campfire," Adam said.

Frank wrote that on the pad. "What else?"

"And go hunting for maybe rabbits."

"Why the 'maybe?'"

"Because maybe we'll see some and maybe we won't."

Frank grinned. "Does it have to be rabbits?"

"No, except in the evening there's more rabbits than javelina or quail."

Frank made more notes. "And I suppose this game is for our supper?"

"Oh no, it's for dinner tomorrow noon when Uncle Seth and Pa get here. Supper is usually leftovers with biscuits."

Frank wrote a few more words. "Then there's the campfire after supper." He smiled at Adam. "Mustn't forget the evening campfire . . . coals banked . . . and finally bedtime." He stood up, slipped the pencil and paper into his shirt pocket, and walked to the end of the compound. He lifted his boots from the brush fence and returned to the cot. Sitting down, Frank pulled his shoes off and his dried boots on. He stood up again. "I believe gathering wood is our next activity."

Suddenly Frank clutched at his leg just below the knee. "I've been stung!" he gasped. "Oh, on the other leg, too." He looked down and slapped at both trouser legs. "Must be wasps . . . burns like fire." He was dancing about slapping at his legs.

Adam jumped up. "Sit on the cot," he ordered.

114

Frank sat down. Quickly Adam yanked the boots off and pulled up the gray trouser legs. A half dozen big red ants curled in vicious bites among the black hairs on Frank's calves. Adam picked them off carefully. "Got to watch out for these, they're mean!" He reached into water barrel for a few drops of water and poured them onto the dust. He rolled the mud into a little ball and plastered bits of it over the angry red welts where the ants had been. He looked up at Frank's sweating face. "This'll take some of the fire out of the bites."

Frank reached for his handkerchief and mopped his forehead. "Where on earth did they come from?"

Adam picked up the boots, turned them upside down, and knocked them together several times. More red ants fell from the boots and struggled through the caliche dust for the brush fence. "Came from the mesquite, most likely," he said, and handed the boots back to Frank.

Frank looked carefully inside his boots again before he pulled them on. He stood up again. "Well, Adam, let's go after the firewood." He reached for the ax beside the tent. "Any special place we find it?" he asked.

Adam waved his arm at the brushland. "It's all over out there, but the sun's too hot now for us to fetch any."

"Of course it's hot, but we have a mail station to run, Adam. As the saying goes, where I come from 'They must hunger in frost that will not work in heat.' Come on, let's go!" He walked briskly toward the fence opening.

Adam sighed and followed Frank. Outside the tent

115

shade, Adam could feel the sun shining uncomfortably hot on his shoulders, which still burned from yesterday's exposure. He padded after Frank, who clumped ahead in his pointed western boots. At a thinly leafed mesquite Frank paused, moved closer in, and swung the ax at the dark rough trunk. The ax blade thudded rhythmically with Frank's vigorous swings. He stopped to wipe the sweat streaming down his face.

Reba had followed them and stood with Adam in the scanty shade of a paloverde.

"That tree's still green, Frank; it won't burn very well." Adam said.

Frank looked up into the network of branches. "Looks dead to me."

"Maybe so, but trees out here look dead when they're not. Drouth makes them drop their leaves; come a rain and they'll green up all over." Adam turned. "There's a dead cedar over yonder." He pointed to a twisted gray tangle of branches. "It chops easy, too."

Frank walked over to the cedar. Adam could see that the back of his shirt was dark where it stuck to his wet body. Frank raised the ax and swung it downward.

The cedar soon lay in firewood lengths, and Adam filled his arms with them. He trudged back to camp, trip after trip. The hot dust under his feet oozed between his bare toes. He wished he could go swimming in the tank.

He paused to wipe his sleeve across his face. He noticed Frank's motions were slower now, and he was stopping frequently to catch his breath. Frank's face was flushed a deep red, too, and the sweat ran freely down his neck. His blue shirt, no longer stiff with starch, hung limp and clinging wet.

"We've got plenty of wood, now, Frank, let's quit." Adam said.

"All right." Frank gave a last blow to a cedar branch. It flipped through the air and landed near a prickly pear. Frank went to retrieve the branch. He looked curiously at the dusty purple fruit growing from the edge of the thick flat cactus pads. "What are these?" he asked.

"Prickly pears," Adam said.

"Can you eat them?"

"Yes, only you've got to watch out for the needles."

"I can see the needles on the plants . . . pretty sharp-looking, all right. But there doesn't seem to be any on this fruit; let's try a couple." Frank reached out, and before Adam could warn him, seized a purple fruit with each hand. The tiny tufts of hairlike needles dotting the dusty purple apples sank deep into his fingers. Frank dropped the fruit in surprise. "Why didn't you warn me, Adam?"

"I did!" Adam said. "You've got to knock the fruit off with a stick. Then you singe the stickers off over the fire."

"Fine time to tell me!" Frank picked at the imbedded needles.

Adam retrieved the ax and cedar branch and walked toward camp. He looked back at Frank limping slowly after him. "Got a rock in your boot?"

Frank raised his eyes from his sore fingers. His face was bright red and puffy under the eyes. He smiled weakly. "No. These confounded boots are rubbing blisters on my toes." Painfully, Frank made his way to the mail station and into the tent.

Adam walked around to his cot in the shade and sank down on it. He was burning up. He had to cool off in the tank. He could hear Frank inside the tent pull his boots off and drop them to the ground. It sounded as though he was changing his clothes again, too.

Adam called through the tent wall. "Let's go swimming and cool off."

Frank didn't answer for a few seconds. When he did, he sounded tired. "You go ahead, Adam. I'm too bushed. Got to rest a bit, then wash out these clothes."

"You can wash your clothes in the tank and cool off at the same time! Come on, the water will make you feel better!"

Again Frank hesitated before he spoke. "The water down there looks pretty muddy to me."

"That's just at the edge, Frank; it's clearer, farther out."

Frank was quiet again, then Adam heard him move slowly off the cot. "All right, you've talked me into it." When he came out of the tent, Frank was wearing a gray striped shirt, fresh dark trousers, and oxford shoes. His arms were full of soiled clothing.

Adam led the way to the tank, and Frank followed, still limping a bit. Near the edge of the pond, Adam stopped by a sage bush, shucked his clothes, and waded in. He could feel the layer of warm water at the surface and cooler water beneath. His bare thighs pushed against the coldness, and he fell forward full length with a shout of relief. He plunged his hot face into the water and, holding his breath, listened to the pulsing gurgle of water entering his ears. He rolled over, blew the water out of his nose, and looked toward the bank. Reba stood on shore, lapping eagerly at the water. Frank had laid his soiled bundle on the ground and was stepping carefully out of his clothes. He folded them neatly and laid them on top of a sage bush.

Frank waded into the tank, balancing himself with his arms. His flushed red face made a sharp contrast with his lean white body. Adam swung his right arm across the surface of the pond and with his palm, sent a long splash of water at Frank. It caught him full in the stomach, and he let out a yell of protest. Frank kicked a returning splash, and the friendly water fight was on.

At last, laughing and breathless, the two waded ashore. Adam seized his own pants and shirt, threw them as far out in the water as he could, and dog-paddled out after them. He dunked them up and down, wrung them out, and splashing ashore, spread them over a sage bush. He returned to the water and wallowed in its sparkling coolness.

Frank, on the other hand, waded gingerly into the pond and methodically scrubbed at the dirt on each garment. He rinsed his clothes thoroughly, and after careful wringing, spread each piece smoothly over the surrounding bushes. It took Frank much longer to wash his clothes, and Adam could see Frank's shoulders were turning red under the fierce glare of the afternoon sun. With the last pair of trousers drying over a sage bush, Frank returned to the water and stretched out to float. The two were silent for a long time while they bobbed on their backs. Ripples lapped at their glistening bodies, which caught and reflected the sun.

It was Frank who finally struggled to his feet and waded ashore. His light body dried quickly in the hot breeze. He turned. "You're right, Adam. I do feel better after that swim."

Adam came slowly out of the water. He watched Frank walk to the bushes and pull on his clothes. Adam could see the puffy red blisters on Frank's toes.

"Why don't you go barefooted, Frank? You'd be a lot more comfortable."

Frank looked down at Adam's leather-brown feet, then at his own tender light ones. "If my feet were as tough as yours, I would." He eased his blistered toes into his socks and shoes.

Adam's body dried quickly in the hot air, too, and he put on his partly wet clothes. He buttoned his shirt and watched Frank check his laundry spread about on the bushes.

Frank looked up. "These clothes aren't dry yet. I'd better leave them awhile longer. They'll be safe here, won't they?"

"Oh sure, Frank, so long as the wind doesn't come up too strong."

"I'll keep a finger in the wind," Frank smiled.

120

"Let's go back to camp and get ready for our evening rabbit hunt."

"We can't hunt until dusk. Rabbits don't come out till then."

"There's plenty we can do meanwhile." Frank limped up the path toward camp. Adam and Reba followed.

When dusk settled, Adam felt almost too tired to hunt. Frank had pushed him all afternoon. They had rearranged the supplies in the tent, cleaned their guns, although Frank's hadn't needed it, and watered down the dust about the camp. Adam had trudged to and from the tank with endless pails of water, which Frank took and threw in glossy fans onto the powdery caliche. Each liquid sheet turned instantly to dull yellow mud when it hit the ground, and sent up puffs of tan dust, which hung in the air a moment, then drifted over the brush fence. They had eaten supper of homebaked bread and leftover fish, and now, with the lavender shadows of the western hills spilling into the brushland, they were leaving the camp, rifles tucked under their arms. Reba followed at their heels.

Frank spotted the first jackrabbit. It stood upright on its hind legs, nibbling at the young shoots of a cat's-claw bush. The thick, thorny branches made a dark background, in the dusk, for the light furry body. Frank raised his gun, aimed, and fired quickly . . . too quickly. The rabbit dropped to its front feet at the same instant the gun went off and, with a flash of white tail, disappeared into the dusk.

Frank chambered another shell in his Hotchkiss Sporting Rifle. "I thought *sure* I had him!" he exclaimed.

"Rabbits are tricky," Adam said. "Got to take your time." He peered carefully about at the darkening landscape. After that gunshot, the rabbits would lie low for a while, but the rattlesnakes wouldn't. He remembered his boots under his cot. He should have put them on, but it was too late now. He turned to Frank. "Maybe if we go down near the tank we might see more rabbits." Adam followed the path, Frank right behind him.

Suddenly Frank paused. "Hold it, Adam." His voice was low and excited. "I think I see a deer!"

Adam stopped in his tracks. "A deer? Where?"

There hadn't been any deer around since he came to the mail station, although he had occasionally seen their tracks in the mud around the tank. Adam peered intently into the fast-gathering darkness.

"There! See? Near the tank. There's several of them." Frank raised his gun.

Adam looked in the direction Frank pointed. Yes, he *could* see the low forms, solid against the surrounding brush. They were motionless now. "Be careful, Frank," he whispered. "Take your time."

"I will," Frank whispered back. He squinted carefully down the gun barrel and slowly squeezed the trigger.

In the sudden flash from the gun barrel, Adam saw one of the forms leap upward and fall slowly out of sight.

"I got him!" Frank was jubilant. He started run-

122

ning through the brush toward the spot where it had fallen.

"Be careful, Frank, be careful," Adam called after him. "Rattlers all around here." But Frank paid little attention to Adam, who was following him more cautiously.

Adam watched the ground for snakes and bumped into Frank, who stood staring at the huddled form on the ground. Adam looked around Frank. It certainly wasn't a deer; it was too small.

Frank moved forward carefully and poked it with his gun barrel.

"What is it?" Adam asked eagerly. "What did you shoot?"

Frank didn't answer for a moment. When he did his voice was almost a squeak.

"My britches, Adam, I shot my britches!" He leaned over and picked up the gray trousers he had hung over the sagebrush to dry that afternoon. In the gloom, Adam could make out a dark bullet hole in the back pocket.

They were both quiet for a moment, then, as though on a signal, they began to laugh. They laughed and laughed. They couldn't stop.

8

IT WAS some minutes before Adam and Frank could control themselves. Frank staggered over and leaned weakly on Adam's shoulder. He wiped his streaming eyes with the gray trousers in his hand. "You know, Adam," he gasped, "that was really stupid of me. I forgot all about leaving these clothes on the bushes."

Adam nodded and held his ribs, sore from laughing. "I plumb forgot about them, too." He chuckled. "They did sort of look like deer."

"They certainly did!" Frank doubled over in another fit of laughter.

After a moment, he straightened up. "Guess I'd better collect my washing." He threw the trousers over his shoulder, tucked his rifle under his arm, and reached for the garments dried into the stiff shapes of the bushes they covered. One shirt had blown to the ground, and he reached toward its white form.

Above the high chirp of the crickets under the sotol and the zoom of the June bugs in the creosote bushes, Adam heard a familiar warning buzz. He peered about

124

the ground. There it was!

"Get back, Frank!" The urgency in Adam's voice halted Frank's hand in midair. Adam pushed past Frank, raised his gun, and aimed at the dark circle lying next to the pale shirt.

"Now, just a minute, Adam!" Frank exclaimed. "I don't want bullet holes in my shirt, too!"

The gun flashed, and the dark coils of a rattler's body thrashed onto the shirt.

Frank shuddered.

The night was suddenly silent, as though the shock waves from the gun had erased all sound. It was Frank who finally broke the silence.

He spoke with sober awe. "How did you know that snake was there, Adam? I didn't hear or see it at all!"

Adam shrugged his shoulders. "Livin' in a rattlesnake run like this, you get to know when they're around."

"A rattlesnake run? What do you mean?" Frank asked.

"Didn't Pa tell you?"

"He mentioned there'd be some snakes out here."

"Mail station's right in the middle of a run, but we're movin' it directly."

"But what *is* a rattlesnake run?"

"Uncle Seth says it's a stretch of land the snakes travel over comin' and goin'." Adam leaned down for the shirt, shook off the rattler's body, and handed the shirt to Frank. "He says it's a kind of road, only wider."

Frank took the shirt and held it gingerly in one

hand. "Where are they going and coming from?" he asked.

Adam tossed his head toward the skyline silhouetted sharply against the last pale streaks of sunset. "Uncle Seth reckons they have dens in those hills over yonder. They come to the tank for water, and for game, like quail and rabbits."

Frank glanced nervously about. "Are they crawling around out here right now?"

"They sure enough are! They don't move much in the day—too hot. But at night you got to watch your step."

"Where can we go to get away from them?"

"Back to camp."

"Aren't the snakes in camp, too? Seems to me if the mail station is inside this . . . rattlesnake run, as you call it, that they'd be there, too."

"They were when I first came out here, but I guess I scared them away. Most snakes don't like livin' right where people are."

"This really *is* the wild west!" Frank exclaimed. "People back east won't believe me when I tell them about this." He shook his head. "But seeing is believing." Frank threw the shirt over his shoulder with the rest of the clothes. "Let's go back to camp, Adam. It's too dark to hunt now, and the thought of all those poisonous rattlesnakes coiling underfoot out here gives me the shivers."

Together they made their way slowly up the path, Adam ahead watching the ground, Frank close behind him peering anxiously over Adam's shoulders. They saw no more rattlers until they passed the mesquite tree near the fence opening.

Frank clutched Adam's shoulder. "There's one, Adam, there by the foot of the tree, see?"

Adam stopped. "Oh, him! He's my friend."

"Your friend? But it's a dangerous rattlesnake!" Adam turned without lifting his gun and shuffled through the opening.

Frank looked in disbelief. "Aren't you going to shoot it?"

Adam looked back. "Nope." He started to pull the brush across the opening.

Frank hurried into the camp. "But why, confound it?"

"Because he did me a favor, that's why!"

Frank scoffed. "No rattlesnake ever did anyone a favor!"

"That one did! He's my mail station guard at night . . . keeps people away so they can't tie their horses to the tree and come in here and bother me!"

Frank threw his head back and laughed. "Who'd ever come out into this God-forsaken place to bother *you*? You're a strange boy, Adam."

Adam wished again that he could tell Frank about Slate and Dugan, but he knew he mustn't.

Frank took his laundered clothing into the tent, then helped Adam throw cedar branches onto the fire. They sat down together before the crackling flames and watched the sparks spiral upward into the dark sky.

128

Reba stretched out between them.

Frank reached over and patted her smooth flanks. "Back home I've got an Irish setter named Red."

"Where's your home?" Adam asked.

"New York City."

"That's a real big town, isn't it?"

"It certainly is."

"Big as San Antone?"

"Bigger than San Antonio—much bigger."

Adam hugged his knees. "That must be mighty big, then."

Frank smiled. "I wish you could see it, Adam, there's no other place like it in the world! Paved streets and new electric lights. Big brownstone houses with thick carpets on the floors . . . silver and china and crystal on the table . . ."

Adam looked up at the sky. "Are the stars this bright in New York?"

Frank followed his gaze. "No, not quite . . . seem dimmer . . . farther away back home. But who needs stars when there's street lights everywhere and houses bright as day inside?" Frank turned and swung his arm toward the brushland. "I tell you, Adam, you're living in the dark ages out here . . . even farther back than that . . . almost to the time of the caveman."

"I'd like to see New York, someday." Adam mused.

Frank leaned forward. "If you ever do, be sure to come and visit me. I'll take you to the museums and theaters and restaurants. I'll show you things that will make your eyes pop . . . Brooklyn Bridge, and electric elevated trains, and the Statue of Liberty out in the Harbor. . . ."

The first wail of the coyotes interrupted Frank and brought him to his feet. "That sounded like a wolf!" he exclaimed.

Adam smiled. "It did to me, too, first time I heard it." He looked up. "Sit down, Frank, it's only a coyote. They come around nearly every night. You'll get used to them."

There was another eerie howl, much nearer. Reba sat up and cocked her ears. Sudden growls and savage snapping erupted just outside of camp. Frank looked toward the tent. "We'd better get our guns and drive them off."

"No need, Frank. They can't hurt us." Adam assured him.

"Sounds to me like they're attacking something out there."

"Probably that javelina carcass I threw out this morning."

Frank limped restlessly back and forth before the fire. He seemed to wince at every bark or growl. Adam knew how he felt. He remembered his own reactions that first night. He looked reassuringly at Frank. "Honest, Frank, they can't hurt a thing!"

"Perhaps so, but those unearthly wails send chills up my spine every time I hear them."

Adam stood up and stretched. "They won't in a day or two." He yawned. "I'm turnin' in, Frank."

Frank looked at Adam in surprise. "How can you sleep with that infernal ruckus going on out there?"

130

Adam grinned. "It's easy when you're tired." He scuffed into the tent and flopped onto his bed. Frank's tall shadow moved back and forth across the tent, but it didn't bother Adam. He was fast asleep in minutes.

A pencil line of light streaked the eastern horizon when Adam awoke the next morning. He raised himself on his elbows and peered through the gloom of the tent at the restless form of Frank stretched out on his cot. He noticed that Frank had laid his clothes at the foot of the bed and placed his shoes neatly beside each other on the ground under the cot. He wondered if he should awaken Frank. If he was to take over the mail station, he should know what sort of game he could find early in the morning.

Adam reached over and touched Frank on the shoulder. Frank groaned.

"Wake up, Frank, it's time to go huntin'," Adam said, shaking Frank's shoulder gently.

Frank started and clutched at his shoulder. "Don't touch me there . . . I'm burning up!" He opened one eye. "What's the matter with you, anyway? This is the middle of the night! Why don't you go back to sleep?"

Adam was patient. "No, Frank, it's mornin'. The game will be everywhere now. This is the time they feed."

"Well, let them feed!" Frank groaned again. "I can't move."

"What's the trouble? Are you sick?" Adam asked anxiously.

Frank opened his tired eyes, puffy with sleep, then

131

closed them again as if the effort was too much. "No, I'm not sick, but I didn't sleep a wink with those coyotes howling all night." He eased himself painfully onto his side. "Besides that, if I *could* move, I doubt that I could stand up, let alone put on a pair of shoes the way my feet feel right now." He was facing the tent wall. "You go ahead, Adam, I've got to get some rest."

Adam reached over for the Winchester and a box of shells. He loaded the gun and slipped out of the tent.

In an hour he was back, with three large jackrabbits dangling from his hand. The dawn glowed red in the east when Adam built the fire up. He went into the tent for the skillet. Frank was sitting on the edge of his cot clad only in his trousers. His head was in his hands, his boots beside him on the bed.

He looked up at Adam and smiled wanly. "Sorry I couldn't make it earlier."

"Don't fret about it." Adam reached for the coffee grinder and beans. "Just you get dressed, and I'll have breakfast ready in a jiffy."

Frank picked up the boots and waved them at Adam. "I can't get these things on. My feet have swelled." He looked critically at the pointed toes. "How do you westerners manage to walk in these things?"

Adam smiled. "Those are ridin' boots, Frank. Nobody here walks in them much."

Frank nodded. "That's understandable." He reached for his shoes under the cot. He started to put one on, then looked up at Adam and grinned. Elaborately, he turned the shoe upside down and tapped it against the

132

other shoe. A large yellowish-brown scorpion tumbled out. It righted itself on the ground and stood at bay, its feet wide apart and its barbed tail arched high over its back. Quickly, Frank drew his feet up onto the cot. He sat staring down at the menacing creature. Finally he looked up. "Adam, what else can happen to a person in this barbarous land? Not only are the elements against the human race, but the flora and fauna as well!"

Adam grinned. "Pa says that out here in the brushland everything either stings, bites, or scratches."

Frank nodded again. "He's right, Adam, he's absolutely right!" Frank reached over the edge of the cot and brought his shoe down on the scorpion with a loud smack. He flipped the crumpled bug far under the bed with the toe of his shoe.

Adam picked up the skillet, bacon, and coffee and went out of the tent. Frank came out in a few minutes, but he still wasn't wearing a shirt. In the early morning sunlight, Adam could see that Frank's shoulders were a dull red.

Frank didn't eat much for breakfast, although Adam made a special effort to please him. With the dishes cleaned up, Adam skinned the rabbits and put them on to stew. Frank stood uncomfortably first on one foot, then the other, only half listening to the instructions Adam was giving him. He picked peevishly at an elusive cactus needle between his fingers. Adam thought Frank seemed strangely quiet. He hadn't once mentioned "the schedule" they were supposed to be following.

When the first feather of dust from Joe Vance's

wagon plumed the horizon, Frank disappeared into the tent. When the mail wagon pulled up, Adam's father leaped to the ground and plowed through the dust to the campfire. He greeted Adam, then looked anxiously about.

"Where's Frank?" he asked.

"Here I am, Mr. Vance." Frank came out of the tent buttoning a fresh shirt.

Adam's father greeted him warmly, and they stood talking until Uncle Seth drove up.

Adam served the rabbit stew, and they all ate. They laughed heartily over Frank's telling of the "deer" shoot the night before.

When they had finished eating, Joe Vance arose. "Well, folks, today we start clearin' brush." He turned to Frank. "We're fixin' to build you another camp over yonder a piece. Adam tell you why?"

Frank smiled wryly. "I found out why last night. I was nearly bitten by one of those rattlesnakes. Adam shot it just in time."

Joe Vance grinned at his son. "He's had lots of practice, I reckon."

Adam started to gather the dishes together. His father looked down at him. "Let them go, Son. I need your help with clearin' brush."

Adam stood up and followed his father, Uncle Seth, and Frank to the wagon. His father reached in and pulled out a brush saw, an ax, and a heavy, long-handled hoe. He handed them all to Frank. "You pack these. The rest of us will handle the palings." He reached

134

in the wagon again and gathered together a stack of the brown pungent freshly-cut cedar stakes, and laid a bundle on his brother's outstretched arms. He handed more to Adam, and pulled out the last bundle for himself. Joe Vance heaved the stakes to his shoulder and led the way through the brush toward the south.

They wound between thickets of coma, whose dark green leaves, blue berries, and dirk-like thorns were powdery with dust. They detoured around tall Spanish daggers, whose fleshy green leaves with tan fibers fraying from the edges stood stiffly erect. Their wicked points protected the dried blossom stalk, bearing seedpods that rattled hollowly in the hot breeze. About the sturdy trunks of the Spanish daggers, dead leaves hung like ragged skirts. Their brittle rustle reminded Adam of dried cornstalks blowing in the wind back home.

Joe Vance stopped at a paloverde with a deep notch in the north side of the green trunk. He turned to Frank. "This is where we start. Thought we'd leave that mesquite in the middle for shade." He pointed to the graceful feathery branches arching over the scrub brush.

Uncle Seth laid the cedar stakes on the ground about four feet apart, outlining a rough oval. While Adam and Frank held the stakes upright, Adam's father drove them into the ground. With the camp outlined by the palings, Adam's father and uncle began cutting the brush inside. Adam dragged the thorny bushes to the fence with the hoe and, together with Frank, heaved them onto the palings. They intertwined the gnarled branches of agarita, low-growing and spiny-leaved, with the thorny limbs of dusty hog plum and switch mesquite.

Frank stopped to unfasten his shirt sleeve from a cat's-claw, whose curved barbs had fastened into him as he heaved the bush onto the palings. "I'll swear, Mr. Vance, everything that grows out here has thorns on it!" he exclaimed.

Joe Vance laughed. "This Texas brushland has more thorns per square inch than a centipede has legs. Used to be fair pasture till it was grazed out. Brush took over after most of the grass was gone."

Frank seized another switch of mesquite and forced it down into the hog plum. "Don't they herd cattle out here?"

Uncle Seth stopped to wipe his face. "Not much any more. This is goat country, now. East a far piece, the brush is full of outlaw critters—longhorns that got away from the regular herds. But here it's goats. They'll eat just about anything, includin' the thorns!"

Adam's father untangled his ax-head from a sage bush. "This stretch right through here is where the brushland turns to desert; got a little bit of everything growin' in it. Out yonder, it's mostly sage and creosote."

Frank shook his head. "I don't see how *anything* can live out here. It's so hot and dry."

Adam grinned as he helped Frank throw a sage bush onto the fence. "*We're* managin' to, aren't we?"

Frank laughed shortly and glanced over his shoulder at the two Vance men. "I wouldn't call it living exactly," he muttered. "Existing would be a better word." He reached into his pocket, pulled out a drenched

136

handkerchief, and mopped his forehead.

Several hours later, Adam's father dragged the last agarita bush to the fence and heaved it on top. "There!" he exclaimed with satisfaction. "We've finished. Didn't think we could manage it in one afternoon." He walked over and trimmed a low-hanging branch from the mesquite tree in the middle of the cleared area. "Tent ought to fit under the tree now." He turned to Frank. "You got yourself a right nice camp here. Hope you enjoy it."

"Mr. Vance." Frank sounded hesitant.

"Yes, Frank?"

"I—I don't know quite how to say this, but . . . I— I can't stay out here."

Joe Vance looked astonished. "Why, what's wrong with it?"

"Oh, there's nothing wrong with the new camp, please don't misunderstand me. It's—it's that I can't do the work."

"You were doin' fine just now."

"It's not that. I thought I could help Adam by teaching him how to be more efficient."

Adam's father looked over at Adam and frowned. "You mean to say my son wouldn't listen to you?"

"Oh no!" Frank protested. "Not that at all."

"Then what's the trouble?"

"Just this. My way of doing things doesn't work in this hostile land, Mr. Vance."

Adam looked up. "But it really isn't hostile, Frank. It's right friendly, once you get to know it."

Frank put his hand on Adam's shoulder. "It isn't

137

hostile to you, Adam. You've learned to live with it."

"You could learn to live with it, too," Adam said.

Frank shook his head. "I'm afraid not. I've lived too long on paved streets and carpeted floors."

"But you've camped before—you said so yourself!"

"Yes, I know, Adam, but where I camped there were cold streams and pine needles—not hot dust and rattlesnakes under foot." He turned to Adam's father. "I'm sorry to disappoint you, Mr. Vance, I truly am, but I'd be useless out here."

Joe Vance looked intently into Frank's earnest eyes. Then he shouldered his ax and turned slowly toward the wagon. "Well, Frank, you know best."

Frank hurried after him, and Adam followed. "Mr. Vance, I've learned a lot from Adam. He knows more about living in the wilderness than I'll ever know. You've raised a bright, resourceful son."

Adam's father turned and smiled. "It's right kind of you to say so, Frank."

"If you want someone really smart to run this station, Mr. Vance," Frank put his hand on Adam's shoulder, "here's your man!"

9

IT WAS mid-afternoon before they returned to camp, watered the horses, and exchanged mailbags. Frank loaded his gear into the wagon bed and climbed up beside Joe Vance. He looked down. "It's been a real pleasure knowing you, Adam. I hope we meet again."

"I enjoyed your company, too. Wish you didn't have to go so soon. I wanted to show you my new fishin' hole."

Frank glanced around the dusty brushland shimmering in the heat. "Now where could you possibly fish out here?"

"In the tank."

"In *that* shallow pond?"

"It's deeper on the other side . . . lots of perch."

Frank shook his head and smiled. "*You* could have a picnic party in the middle of a desert, Adam. I don't see how you work such magic."

"There isn't any magic to it; it's just knowin' where—"

Frank raised his hand. "Ah! *That's* the magic!

Knowing where . . . and how, and what, and when, and who! I take my hat off to the great wizard Adam." Frank swept his hat off and bowed in mock solemnity.

Joe Vance smiled, clucked to the horses, and they were off. Adam watched until the wagon was swallowed up in the spiraling yellow dust plumes.

With everyone gone, loneliness settled on Adam like the powdered caliche on the brush fence. He remembered, with a twinge, how angry he had felt when Frank first arrived yesterday afternoon. Despite his strange eastern ways, Frank had been fun. Adam smiled when he thought of the long afternoon swim, the evening hunt, and the campfire together. Somehow sharing these pleasures had been a lot more satisfying than keeping them to himself. He would miss Frank.

Turning, Adam glanced southeast toward the horizon. A long low bubble of dust boiled slowly toward the mail station. It didn't move high nor fast enough to be men on horseback, but progressed in a slow rolling motion. Maybe it was a dust storm. Adam cocked his head on one side and listened; sometimes you could hear the roar of the wind before it arrived. Perhaps he had better drive the tent stakes deeper, he thought. Then he smiled. Was it his imagination, or did he hear bleating? It must be a flock of sheep, or a herd of goats.

The sound of bleating grew louder, and in the edge of the dust roll, he could make out the forms and quick movements of goats moving through the brush. They must be headed for the tank, he thought.

Adam ran outside the station to see them better.

140

Reba ran barking at his heels. The herder appeared suddenly from around a mesquite thicket. He walked slowly ahead of the tan and white animals, his head bent forward. He was a short, slender man with a dusty sombrero pulled low over his face and a frayed gray blanket folded over his shoulder. He wore a faded blue shirt and trousers much patched and many sizes too big for him. Dusty huaraches were tied on his feet. He shuffled toward the mail station, and Adam could see, slung over his other shoulder, the familiar water gourd and deep canvas food satchel of a Mexican herder. In the deep shadow of his sombrero the man's bronze-colored face showed the unmistakable wide cheekbones and thick nose of generations of Yaqui blood.

Adam quieted Reba and stepped forward. *"Buenas tardes, señor!"* he greeted.

The goat herder stopped and raised his head. His black eyes drilled Adam.

"Buenas tardes, señor," Adam repeated, and he smiled warmly at the goat herder.

The little man continued slowly forward, studying Adam as he came. He stopped in front of Adam, his eyes on a level with the boy's. Adam looked into the dark face, wrinkled like the instep of an old leather boot and realized the Mexican was very old.

The goat herder dipped his head. *"Buenas tardes, mi amigo!"* His voice was soft and musical. "You favor me by speaking my tongue. I am grateful."

Adam grinned. "It is nothing, señor. Juanita, our housekeeper, taught me to speak Spanish when I was

141

very young."

The wrinkles in the old man's face deepened and he smiled. "Tell me, *mi amigo*, what are you doing so far out in the chaparral?"

Adam waved at the camp. "I am caring for this mail station. My name is Adam Vance."

The herder swept his hat from his head and held it against his chest while he bowed low. "Your servant, Feliz Mariano. I am taking this small *cabrío* north to the plain. Perhaps there is more forage up there for them . . . but with this drouth, *quién sabe?*"

"There is a tank a little distance away where you may wish to water your goats."

Feliz smiled. "They know of it already. Early this afternoon, Pepe, their leader, smelled the water. See? They follow him to it now."

Adam watched the bleating goats jostle each other as they trotted down the path toward the tank. Reba ran after them, sniffing at their heels.

Feliz turned. "I must follow them, too. My gourd is nearly empty."

"Allow me to fill it from my water barrel, señor. The water in the tank becomes muddied quickly."

The herder shook his head. "Thank you, *mi amigo*, but Feliz needs only the thick pad of the tuna cactus to clarify the *agua*."

"I do not understand, señor."

"Come, follow me. I will show you." Feliz shuffled down the path.

Adam hurried after him. The thick haze of dust

that hung in the warm air above the path was heavy with the odor of goats. At the tank, he saw at least fifty of the mottled tan, white, and brown animals ankle-deep in the sticky caliche, shoving each other aside for drinking places.

Feliz removed the blanket from his shoulder and laid it over a sage bush. He lifted the water gourd off and pulled the wide band of the bulky food satchel over his head, laying the satchel and gourd beside the blanket. Feliz leaned over to rummage in the satchel, and Adam saw a long flash of sunlight glint along the sharp edge of a machete tucked into his belt. It had been hidden under the blanket until now. From the satchel, Feliz drew a squat cooking pot by its bail. He set it on the ground while he untied the thongs of his dusty huaraches and rolled up his trouser legs. With the pot dangling from one hand, the herder pushed the goats aside and waded out into the water.

Feliz smiled back at Adam. "Ah, how good the *agua* feels to my tired feet. I have walked very far today." He leaned over where the water was still fairly clear, dipped the pot full, and splashed back to shore. He set the pot on the ground and disappeared into the brush in the direction of a prickly pear thicket. In a moment he returned, a fat cactus pad speared on the end of his machete. He dropped the pad into the cooking pot with a splash, then, as the cactus bobbed about in the water, deftly sliced the pad into strips with the sharp point of his machete.

Adam squatted on his heels in the late afternoon

143

shade of a creosote bush and watched, while Reba flopped beside him. "Why do you do that, señor?" he asked.

"The tuna leaf will cause the mud to fall to the bottom. Then I shall pour the clarified water into my gourd." Feliz sat down Indian-fashion beside Adam. "The tuna cactus is useful in many ways. It is the gift of God, you know."

"Are not all the plants gifts of God?" Adam asked.

"*Sí*, but the tuna is a special gift. You do not know the story?"

"No, señor."

Feliz settled himself, his bright eyes on Adam's face. His hands moved like the shuttle of a loom among his soft words.

"When the earth was still young and man could talk with God and the beasts, there lived in Chihuahua, a poor *paisano*, Juan Ortez, who raised a few goats and a small patch of *maiz* and *frijoles* near his little house to feed his family. A drouth descended upon the land. The goats died. The *maiz* and the *frijoles* withered on the stalk. Soon there was no food left.

"Juan rose early one morning and said to his wife, Maria, 'Bring me my sling and water gourd. Today I shall hunt in the desert. Perhaps I can bring back a quail, or a rabbit, or even a deer for us to eat.'

"Maria brought his sling and water gourd. 'May you go with God,' she said, as she handed them to him.

"Juan had not traveled many *varas* from his home when he saw a tiny quail resting in the shade of a

144

guajillo bush. Quietly, he bent down and selected a smooth stone. He fitted it into his sling, and was about to raise his arm to swing the stone about his head, when the quail cried out in a pitiful voice, 'Spare me, Juan, spare me!'

" 'Why should I spare you?' Juan asked. 'My family is hungry.'

"The quail spread its wings. 'There is hardly enough meat on me to keep my feathers from sticking to my bones, let alone feed your family. Over behind that coma bush you will find a rabbit who would make a much better meal than I.'

"Juan looked at the tiny quail and lowered his sling. 'Sí, you are right. You would hardly be worth the plucking.' He crept toward the coma bush where a large rabbit lay panting in the shade.

"The rabbit saw him and jumped up. 'Oh, Juan, you do not want me for your dinner.'

" 'Why not?' asked Juan. 'My family is hungry.'

"The rabbit stood on his hind legs. 'Observe, I am too thin . . . nothing but fur and bones.'

"Juan looked at the slender rabbit. 'Sí, you are right. You would hardly be worth the skinning.'

"The rabbit pointed to a clump of coma and granjeno bushes. 'In that thicket lies a deer. He would make a much better meal for your family than I.'

"Juan searched the ground for a larger stone, then crept toward the thicket.

"Suddenly the thorny bushes shook violently and a small deer leaped out with a snarling coyote right be-

145

hind it. Juan swung his sling and let the stone fly. But instead of striking the deer, his stone struck the coyote, which fell to the ground dead, while the frightened deer disappeared into the chaparral.

"Juan looked sadly at the beast on the ground. His family could not eat the coyote, for everyone knows it is a dog of the devil. He turned to walk away when a voice spoke suddenly from the thicket: 'Juan Ortez.'

"Juan looked about. He could see no one. He grew pale and fell to his knees, for he knew it must be the voice of God speaking from the thicket. His own voice trembled. '*Sí, mi Dios,* what do you wish?'

"The voice was kind. 'You are a good man, Juan, for you have spared my creatures and destroyed only the dog of the devil. For this, you and your family shall not go hungry.'

"'But where shall I find food?' Juan asked.

"'Return to your house. Nearby you will find a plant growing, which will furnish your family with food and drink so long as you are willing to work for it.'

"'*Gracias, mi Dios, gracias*!' Juan rose and hurried back to his little house. Maria ran out to greet him, and he told her of his adventure. Together they looked about. Near the door of the house, they saw a great tuna cactus standing, its fat green pads covered with bright fruit. They hurried over to it. Maria looked at the plant, then turned and smiled at Juan. 'He is right. We shall have to work for our food. See how God has studded the plant with thorns.'"

Feliz chuckled to himself and leaned forward to peer into the pot of water. Adam leaned forward, too, and gazed at the tiny squares of green prickly pear pads floating on the surface. He looked beneath them and saw that the yellow sediment had indeed settled to the bottom. The water was clear. Feliz dipped the cactus pieces gently from the pot and poured the liquid into the smooth hollow gourd, which he held by its short neck. He turned and offered the gourd to Adam. "Drink, *mi amigo*," he smiled.

Adam knew he must not refuse this friendly gesture, for the Mexican herder would consider such a refusal an insult. He reached for the gourd and drank a few sips of the tepid water. It was surprisingly sweet. He handed it back to Feliz. "*Gracias*, señor, it is indeed delicious."

Beaming, the herder took the gourd, lifted it to his lips, and drank slowly in big audible gulps. With an "Ah-h-h!" of satisfaction, he wiped the back of his hand across his mouth, fitted the little goatskin cap over the top of the gourd, and set it in the shade of the bush beside him. Twisting around, he reached into his food satchel and pulled a round napkin-covered package from its depth. He laid it on his lap, unfolded the corners, and revealed a small pile of tortillas. He offered them to Adam. "*Por favor*, share my humble food."

Adam reached out and peeled a tortilla from the stack. "*Gracias*, señor." He grinned and bit into the thin pancake with its unmistakable corn flavor. "It has been days since I have enjoyed a tortilla. Juanita makes delicious ones for me at home." Adam waved the limp cake in his hand. "I have missed these out here at the mail station."

Feliz deftly rolled a tortilla into a tube shape and bit off a piece. He shook his head and gestured with his free hand at the tortillas in his lap. "These are too old to be tasty. My daughter, Teresa, made them yesterday when I stopped at her home."

Reba sniffed at the hoofs of a large tan goat that nibbled at a dry *perezia* blade close by. The goat turned and butted playfully at the dog. Reba stuck her tail between her legs and ran back to Adam. He patted her reassuringly and glanced about. "Are these your own goats, señor?"

"Ah, no, *mi amigo*," the herder smiled. "Feliz Mariano is much too poor to own fifty goats. I drive them to pasture for Señor Stearns. His *rancho* is near Rio Verde. Every ten days his foreman, Alfredo Ruiz, rides out with supplies for me—a few pounds of beans, a little flour— that is all. I hunt for the rest."

"How can you hunt when you have no gun?"

"I need no gun. I have my machete and my sling." Feliz reached into the satchel again and pulled out a sturdy leather thong. A supple piece of cowhide, oval-shaped, the size of a hen's egg, was attached in the middle.

"Can you really hit a rabbit with that?" Adam asked.

"*Sí*, I have hit many."

"Will you show me how?"

"With pleasure, Adam. But we must wait until the evening." Feliz bit into another tortilla and smiled at Adam. "It is pleasant to have a companion to talk with while one eats. A herder's life is a lonely one. Often Señor Ruiz is the only person I speak to for days."

Adam nodded. "I know loneliness, too, señor."

Feliz frowned and shook his head. "It is not right that a *muchacho* should be left alone."

"Oh, but I do not mind it anymore. I can hunt in the chaparral with my rifle, and fish in the tank. Besides, I see my father once a day." Adam watched two white goats nibble daintily at the dusty shoots of a coma bush. "I have learned a few things since I have been out here by myself."

Feliz nodded. "The wilderness of God can teach us much."

A turtledove, with noisy whir of wings, settled on the topmost branch of the coma bush and cooed softly. Feliz pointed at the bird. "Do you know what the dove is saying?"

"No, señor."

" '*Comer comas, comer comas*, I want to eat comas berries, I want to eat comas berries.' "

Adam laughed. "It *does* sound a little like that."

Feliz' musical voice imitated the sad call of the gray dove perched on the coma branch. It cocked its head from side to side and listened. When Feliz finished, the dove, with a high-pitched whir of wings that sounded to Adam like a feathery laugh, rose swiftly and flew across the tank and into the chaparral.

149

A big tan and white goat that had been browsing close by clattered over to Feliz on its sharp little hoofs and nuzzled into the herder's shoulder. Feliz reached up and patted the sleek neck of the animal. "This is Pepe. He is a smart goat. He knows the chaparral well and can lead the herd to a guajillo thicket like a bee to the blossom."

Pepe explored under Feliz' arm. The herder grinned. "He desires a bonus for leading the herd to water." The goat reached out and boldly nibbled at the edge of Feliz' straw sombrero. Instantly, Feliz was on his feet. "*Chihuahua!*" he exclaimed and waved his arms angrily at Pepe. "No treat for one who would consume my sombrero. *Vamos*, you brother of the devil!" The goat trotted off bleating indignantly.

Adam arose. The sun was squinting over the western hills, drawing long shadows across the brushland. "Señor, we must find a safe place for your goats to bed down. There are too many rattlesnakes around this tank at night."

Feliz smiled. "That is a good omen—many rattlesnakes. It will rain soon."

"You do not understand, señor. This is a road for the snakes. They come down from their dens in the hills to feed about the tank."

The herder smiled again and shook his head. "There are no roads for the rattlesnake. He comes and goes where he pleases."

"Yes, but there are many more rattlesnakes right

150

around here than other places in the chaparral. My Uncle Seth says—"

Feliz came close and shook his dark finger under Adam's nose. "Listen, *mi amigo,* Feliz Mariano has spent his life in the wilderness of God. He knows much about the signs of the weather." He emphasized his words with quick nods. "Many rattlesnakes means rain soon."

Adam realized it was useless to argue with the old herder. Yet he must convince Feliz that the goats should be bedded down outside the rattlesnake run. He remembered the clearing for the new station they had finished that afternoon. It would be a fine place for the goats. He turned to Feliz. "Señor, we have a clearing surrounded by a brush fence nearby where you are welcome to bed down your goats."

"*Gracias,* Adam, I shall herd them there at once." Feliz slung his blanket, water gourd, and food satchel over his shoulder. He waved his arms and shouted, gathering the animals together.

Adam chased two into the flock and joined Feliz. "Why do you not have a dog to help you?"

Feliz shook his head. "Dogs move the goats too fast. The goats grow thin, and Señor Stearns grows angry." The old herder drew from his belt a flat stick about three feet long which was rounded at the ends. "This is one of my herders. Watch." He threw the stick toward a goat who had strayed from the flock. The stick clattered along the ground, turning cartwheels as it went, and barely grazed the animal. The startled goat turned and hurried into the safety of the flock. Feliz retrieved the stick and returned to Adam. "My sling is the other herder, but out here in the chaparral I do not use it. A stone skipped along the ground is easily deflected by the bushes into the herd and likely to injure a *cabrito*."

When they reached the new clearing, Adam helped Feliz drive the goats into the compound. Together they piled the brush high to enclose the animals.

Feliz stepped back. "That is a fine corral. But tell me, *mi amigo*, why do you need it out here in the brushland?"

Adam knew his explanation would seem silly to the old herder, who refused to believe there was such a thing as a rattlesnake run. Adam watched the goats in the center of the clearing stand on their hind legs to reach the mesquite beans hanging from the branches of the shade tree. "The other station does not have a tree to shade it during the day," he answered. It did not sound convincing, but Feliz seemed satisfied with the answer.

Feliz smiled. "My goats will not need to be guarded tonight."

"Then come and share my camp, señor. It is but a short distance away." Adam was eager to hear more of the old herder's stories.

"*Gracias, mi amigo.* But first let me chop the heart from this sotol to roast in the coals." Feliz stopped before a large sotol crown and drew his machete. With vigorous whacks, he chopped at the leaves, exposing the large white center, which he carefully cut out and

152

dropped into his food satchel. "Now I will show you how my sling will kill a rabbit."

With eyes lowered, the old herder searched the ground in the gathering shadows. He reached down and selected a smooth round rock the size of a small egg from the dusty path. Turning, he walked back toward the tank. Adam wished he had his gun with him. Feliz might be very good at hitting a rabbit with a stone, but what would he do if a rattler struck at him? Adam called Reba, and together they followed the spry little Mexican, who moved as stealthily as a bobcat among the thickets of prickly pear, guajillo bushes, and cat's-claw.

Near the tank, the old herder stopped and held up his hand. He put a finger to his lips, and Adam drew close. "Good fortune is with us," Feliz whispered. "See? Beside the *cedro*? An armadillo!"

Adam strained to see the shadowy shape rooting in the cedar needles. How could Feliz possibly kill an armadillo? he wondered. The stone would surely bounce off that tough leathery armor that protected the animal from head to foot. Everyone knew the only soft place was its belly, and that was close to the ground.

Feliz put his hands to his mouth and gave a strange quavering call. Adam could see the shadowy form stand still for a moment. Then it rose on its hind legs and swayed slowly from side to side. Quickly, Feliz fitted the stone into the center of the sling. The leather thong whirred around his head for a moment, and the stone whistled through the air. There was a thud, followed by

153

scrambling noises under the cedar. Feliz darted forward, and Adam followed. The machete flashed dully in the twilight and Feliz stood up, hands on his hips.

The herder's white teeth gleamed in the shadow of his sombrero. He gestured at the animal lying beneath the cedar. It was fully as large as Reba. "Ah, a fine big one, is it not?"

Adam saw the faint pink oval of the armadillo's belly, like the cut half of a large watermelon. The animal lay rocking slightly on its hard round-shelled back. "How did you do that, señor?" Adam asked in awe.

"It is simple, my friend. Strange noises make the armadillo stand up to see better, for his eyes are very bad. It is then that his belly is exposed, and one can kill him easily with a stone." The old herder bent forward and dragged the large animal out from under the cedar by its thick rough-sheathed tail. "Come, let us build a good fire. We shall feast tonight, eh, *mi amigo*?"

10

ADAM started up the path for the mail station. He could hear the soft slap of Feliz' huaraches following him in the dusk. Feliz was dragging the armadillo by the tail. Its armored back made a smooth trail in the powdered caliche. Adam grinned to himself. Was it only twenty-four hours ago that he had come this same way with Frank? What a difference between his companions of the two evenings—Frank, who jumped at every moving shadow on the ground; Feliz, who utterly ignored the rattlesnake warning. Yet Adam liked them both.

If only Frank had been willing to stay a little longer, he would have met Feliz, who lived with such graceful ease in the wilderness Frank called a "hostile land." Adam had grown to like the brushland, and he had wanted Frank to like it, too. Feliz, with his resourcefulness and love of even thorny cactus, could have helped show Frank that when one becomes familiar with one's surroundings, there is little to fear. Perhaps, Adam thought, he would find the man-made arroyos of New

York City as forbidding as Frank had found his land.

Inside the mail station, Adam quickly started the fire. With the flames leaping upward, he went back to pull the brush across the opening after Feliz had dragged the armadillo nearer the fire. The flickering light glinted on the sharp machete in Feliz' hand. Adam watched him turn the armadillo over and, with quick strokes, cut the shell away from around the neck. He flipped it over on its back again and cut down the hind legs and around the tail. With his feet on either side of the shell, the old herder pulled upward on the tail, cutting the body away from the shell. He lifted the body out carefully, removed the entrails with a few more strokes, and held the carcass up while Adam poured several dippers of water over it.

Feliz handed the animal to Adam, reached into the satchel, and brought out a sturdy leather thong. He attached the thong to the tail of the armadillo, which Adam was still holding. Feliz drew the metal rod from the supports on either side of the fire and tied the other end of the thong to the middle of the rod. Together, they carried the armadillo to the fire and fitted the rod into the upright supports.

Adam stepped back and watched the armadillo, suspended over the coals, turn slowly in the heat, winding and unwinding on the heavy leather thong. He turned to Feliz. "You know many things, señor. I would have spitted the carcass and spent much time turning it by hand."

Feliz smiled. "This is a lazy man's way of roasting

meat. Now I can sit by the fire and enjoy myself." He dropped to his knees and pulled the satchel and water gourd from his shoulders. From the satchel he lifted the sotol heart, raked the coals aside with the tip of his machete, and dropped the heart in. He pushed the coals back around the sotol. Wiping his hands on his knees, he spread the gray blanket on the ground and leaned back on it. Adam sat down with Reba stretched between them.

Feliz lifted his sombrero and ran his fingers through his thick gray hair. "Now I am *contento*. My goats are safe within the corral, there is meat cooking over a warm fire, I have a fine companion to talk to, and the sky is clear overhead."

Adam glanced up. "The stars are indeed bright tonight, señor. See how the Star of the North glitters."

The old herder looked up. *"La estrella del norte* belongs to *Dios*. See how the *corrida* creeps slowly around, guarding it from man and beast?"

"Which is the *corrida*, señor?"

The Mexican pointed to the Big Dipper. "The stars close by. See, the great wagon and the three workmen standing right behind the wagon tongue? There is the foreman, that bright star closest to *la estrella del norte*. He directs the other *vaqueros* and the great *remuda* they drive about the North Star."

Adam located the various stars Feliz mentioned and watched their slow movement in the quiet night. Only the sizzle of fat dripping from the slowly turning armadillo broke the stillness. Suddenly Adam sat up. "But señor, the wagon is moving backward!"

"*Sí*, Adam. The great wagon is dragging its tongue. That is because all things are reversed in the heavens, which we see only at night, from the things on the earth, which we see only in the day."

"Except the Milky Way, señor. It does not move around."

"If you mean *el camino de San Pedro,* the pathway of St. Peter, *sí.* It always goes from south to north." Feliz sat up and looked intently at the sky. "Ah, *mi amigo,* another sign! See how much brighter the stars of *San Pedro*'s pathway are in the south? They are pointing to the north, from which direction the wind will blow very soon."

"Do you think a norther is on its way?"

Feliz shrugged his shoulders. *"Quien sabe?* The season for them draws near. If the moon were shining, we could count the stars in *la casa de luna,* that great circle that surrounds it, and we would know the number of days until rain. But it will rain when God wills." Feliz leaned back again.

"It is strange, señor, I do not hear the coyotes tonight."

"It is not strange. They wait to sing on the hills tomorrow after the sun has risen."

"Why is that?"

"It is another sign of rain."

"But if the coyote is the son of the devil, how does he know the will of God that it should rain?"

The old herder laughed. "You are very *perceptivo,*

mi amigo. It is because *el coyote* is cunning—as cunning as an eagle with its shoes off. He can talk to the fences and they will let him through. He can sing to *el gallo,* and the rooster will fall off his perch."

"How did *el coyote* become so clever, señor?" Adam asked. He was sure Feliz would have a story for this, and he was not wrong.

Feliz smiled. "It happened in the beginning of time, when *el coyote, el perro* (the dog), and *el lobo* (the wolf), were brothers. They lived together in a great cave that overlooked a winding road. One day two strangers came along the road arguing violently. They stopped just below the cave to rest, and the three brothers overheard the strangers' conversation.

" 'But my master brings the sun up every morning,' the first stranger said.

" 'And I take it away every night,' the second said.

" 'My master rules the day,' the first said.

" 'And I rule the night,' the second said.

" 'My master brings life to the earth; therefore he is the greatest of all masters,' the first concluded.

" 'And I bring death to the earth. That proves my superiority,' the second said.

"*El coyote* looked at his two brothers and whispered, 'Do you know who these strangers are?'

"His brothers shook their heads.

" 'They are *San Pedro* and *Don Diablo.*'

" 'It is strange that they should be traveling together,' observed *el lobo.*

" 'It is not strange at all,' *el coyote* said. 'Good and bad

159

go hand in hand everywhere.'

"The two strangers looked up and saw the three brothers.

"The first stranger stood up. 'Observe, *Don Diablo,* here are three who can settle our argument. Tell me, good brothers, would you not rather follow my master who brings the sun up every morning?'

" 'Follow me, and I will show you how to take the sun away every night,' *Don Diablo* said.

" 'And *my* master will rule the day for you.'

" 'And *I* will show you how to rule the night.'

" 'You will feel the gentle rain and warm sunshine that *my* master brings.'

" 'I will teach you how to predict the rains and bring hot winds to dry them up.'

" 'My master will bring you life. Is he not the greatest master?'

" 'And I will show you how to bring death. Is this not a greater knowledge?'

"The three brothers looked at one another. *El perro* spoke first. 'I judge *San Pedro*'s master the greatest, for I would live in the day and hunt in the sunlight.'

"*El coyote* smiled. 'You did not listen well, my brother. True, *San Pedro*'s master rules the day, but observe, *Don Diablo* offers to show one *how* to rule the night. *San Pedro*'s master does not offer this knowledge. I would follow *Don Diablo*.'

"*El lobo* shook his head. 'I cannot decide, for I like the day and the night. I like the rain and the hot wind. I like life and death.'

160

"The two strangers smiled up at the brothers. *San Pedro* held out his hand. 'Come, *perro*, follow me. I will give you a home in the sun with people who will care for you and for whom you may care.'

" 'Come, *coyote*,' *Don Diablo* beckoned. 'Follow me, and I will teach you all the cunning tricks that will make you master of the night.' And so it was *el perro* followed *San Pedro*, and *el coyote* followed *Don Diablo*, leaving *el lobo* to sit in the cave by himself."

Feliz leaned toward the fire. With the tip of his machete, he turned the steaming sotol heart and poked tentatively at the roasting armadillo. "We shall eat soon," he nodded. "The armadillo cooks quickly."

Adam rose. "Then I shall grind the coffee beans."

"Coffee?" The old herder's face beamed in the firelight. "That is a great treat for Feliz Mariano. The *agua* is his daily drink."

With fragrant coffee bubbling over the coals, Adam brought the plates and cups from the tent. Feliz cut the sotol heart in half, placed it on the plates, and sliced the sizzling meat from the armadillo. Adam poured the coffee, and together they sat down to eat. The sotol heart tasted to Adam like a watery sweet potato. The armadillo meat reminded him of the javelina he had roasted.

When they had finished eating, Adam cleaned the plates and cups and put them away. He returned to the campfire and found Feliz humming to himself. The tune was a familiar one. He had heard Juanita sing it at home. "Is that *La Jesucita* you hum?" he asked.

The old herder smiled at Adam. "*Sí*, you know it?"

161

Adam nodded and sat down cross-legged beside Feliz. "Juanita taught me the words."

"Then we shall sing it together." Feliz leaned back on his elbows, and the air filled with his rich tenor that gave no sign of the herder's age. Adam joined him as he sang:

"Come, let us go to the dance, see how lovely,
Where twenty lanterns are burning so brightly.
Come where the dancers are swaying so lightly.
See how they step to the rhythm of the dance.
So favor me, Jesucita,
And dance with only me.
You know that I am your lover;
My heart beats just for thee."

Feliz laughed when they finished. "For a *muchacho* you have a strong voice. Do you know *Cielito Lindo*?"

Adam nodded and started singing "*De la Sierra Morena, Cielito Lindo . . .*"

Feliz sang with him. The joy in the song seemed to Adam to fill his very bones. He turned to Feliz grinning. "Singing makes me happy. Does it not make you feel the same?"

"*Sí*, when the belly fills with food, the heart fills with song. Even *el coyote* will tell you this." Feliz reached over and threw another mesquite branch on the fire. With the sparks that swirled upward, his voice rose in the gay *Los Animales,* and Adam joined in the refrain "*Ay eso sí es verdad*! Ah, that is certainly true!" They sang *Los Diez Perritos,* the ten little dogs, and *El Casamiento del Piojo y la Pulga,* the wedding of the flea and the

163

louse. It was late when they stopped singing, but Adam didn't care. He would not have to hunt tomorrow, for there was plenty of armadillo left. Adam lay back on the ground and put his hands under his head. He gazed up at the Pleiades, the seven stars that clustered above him in a faint cloud of light. "What do you call that constellation, señor?" he asked pointing. "The stars that gather close together?"

Feliz tilted his head back. "Those are 'the little goats.' They have no herder except *Dios*." He smiled and rose stiffly to his feet, "But the goats in this corral do have a herder, and he had better see that they rest safely." The old man reached into the fire for a burning branch. "I must go to them now." He started away from the fire, holding the blazing mesquite stick.

Adam jumped to his feet. "Wait, señor, I will get my gun and go with you. It is not safe to go alone with so many rattlesnakes about."

Feliz shrugged. "They will not harm me. I have but to wave this burning stick in their faces and they will turn away."

Adam hurried into the tent and felt along the wall for the Winchester. The old man could be right, but Adam didn't want him to take any chances. He seized the gun and ran out to help Feliz pull the brush aside. Outside of the mail station, Feliz held the burning stick near the ground and swung it slowly from side to side. Together, they threaded their way between the brush toward the new clearing. Reba trotted at their heels. Adam held his gun ready, should he hear the warning

164

buzz of a rattler.

At the new clearing, the herder held the branch high above his head and peered in at the goats. Adam could see the goats staring back. Their luminous eyes, clustered about the mesquite tree in the center, seemed to hang in space, unattached to their bodies. Feliz listened for a moment. The goats' sleepy blether seemed to reassure him. "All is well with them," he said, and turned back toward the mail station.

Adam sighed with relief when they entered the camp and pulled the brush together again. They had met no rattlers, thank goodness! Maybe Feliz was right. Maybe the rattlesnakes *did* turn away from the burning torch, but Adam was too sleepy to wonder why. Yawning, he banked the fire and turned to Feliz. "You are welcome to use my cot and my tent, señor."

The herder smiled and bowed slightly, shaking his head. "You are very kind, *mi amigo*, but Feliz Mariano needs only the mat of the earth and the covering of the heavens to bring him sleep." The old herder lifted the gray blanket, shook it slightly, and drew it nearer the coals that glowed faintly under the layer of ashes. He lowered himself to the blanket. "*Buenas noches, mi amigo*," he said and, lying down, rolled up like a cocoon.

"*Buenas noches*, señor," Adam answered. He stumbled into the tent, put the gun in the corner, fell onto his cot, and was asleep before the tent flap had stopped swaying.

The crackle and snap of flames awakened Adam. Alarmed, he sat up in the pale dawn. He wondered if the brush fence had caught on fire. He fumbled with the tent flap and looked out. Feliz was hanging the coffeepot over the fire to heat the left-over coffee. The old man glanced quickly at Adam and smiled. *"Buenos días, mi amigo."*

Adam rubbed his eyes. *"Buenos días,* señor. Is it morning already?"

"Sí, and time for Feliz Mariano to lead his goats to the hills. The weather changes very soon. See the sheep in the sky?" He pointed to the high cirrus clouds that filled the dawning heavens like a pink tent top of watered silk.

Adam shuffled outside rubbing his tousled head. He looked about for the hens. They scratched industriously in the dust near the fence opening. "There may be some eggs in the brush, señor. I will look." Adam searched the nests the hens had made and returned to the fire with four eggs.

Feliz' face wrinkled with a delighted smile. *"Magnífico!* Now we shall have *huevos a caballo,* eggs on horseback."

Adam brought the skillet out of the tent and Feliz poured a little water into it, letting it heat till it steamed. With a flourish, he broke each egg and dropped it into the water.

Adam watched the transparent eggwhites slowly solidify and the yolks glaze over in the bubbling water. He hurried into the tent for the plates and cups and the tin with a few biscuits in it. Together, they sat down to eat. It was a pleasant breakfast, even though the biscuits were hard and the coffee bitter. Adam glanced at the serene face of the old Mexican. Never had he met

166

such a kind and understanding person. How he wished Feliz could stay! There was so much Adam wanted to learn from him.

Suddenly the sun rose and sent its rays deep into the brushland. From the distant hills, the long wail of a coyote floated across to the mail station. Another "yip, yip, yip, ah-o-o-o" followed, and still another.

Feliz put down his cup and plate. "See? Did I not say *el coyote* would sing from the hills this morning? He tells us it will rain very soon." The old herder turned toward the hills. "Sing, *amigos*, sing. For rain will bring new shoots to the chaparral, and my goats will grow fat, and Señor Stearns will grow happy."

"But señor, how can you tell when the coyotes sing of rain?"

"It is simple, *mi amigo*. If they sing in the brushland before dawn, it means nothing. But if they sing on the hills after the sun has arisen, then they sing only of rain." The old herder rose. "I must lead my goats to the protection of the hills. The cold winds that follow the storm are bad for them." Feliz folded his blanket. He cut a few strips of meat from the armadillo, wrapped them in the napkin, and stuck them into his satchel, while Adam filled his gourd from the water barrel.

Adam pushed aside the brush, and together they followed the faint trail to the new clearing. The goats were bleating loudly, anxious to leave their pen. They milled about the entrance, and as soon as Adam and Feliz had pulled the brush aside, they poured out into the chaparral like water out of a bottle. Pepe trotted toward the tank. He kicked his heels in the air, and the herd followed suit.

Feliz smiled. "Pepe knows that they may not see another tank for some days."

At the tank the goats stamped deep in the mud and shook themselves as they jostled each other for a place to drink. Feliz turned to Adam, his face happy. "See how they shake themselves as though they were wet? That is another sign of rain. It will be hard to manage them today, for they know, too, that there will be new green leaves on the guajillo bush and the cenizo will blossom like a lavender cloud."

Adam wiped the sweat from his forehead with the back of his hand. Not a breeze moved the dusty air. Despite the high clouds that made the sunlight hazy now, it seemed stiflingly hot. "I hope it rains soon, señor. This is the hottest day since I've been in the brushland."

"Don't worry, Adam. It will rain before the sun sets." The old herder squinted at the northern edge of the sky. "See *la vaca*, the cow, that dark cloud that spreads from the north?"

Adam saw the flat storm clouds, steely blue, creeping over the horizon. He had known the fierceness of these storms before—"blue northers" they called them —when the temperature dropped rapidly, often to freezing. One never knew whether it would be a wet norther with rain, or a duster without rain. But the wind would blow hard with either kind of storm. Adam hoped that Feliz would reach the hills beforehand.

"I must gather my goats and leave now." Feliz

drew his herding stick from his belt and waved it in the air. He shouted at the goats and drove them from the tank into a tight group. He turned to Adam. "May the storm treat you gently, *mi amigo*." The dark eyes in the leathery face were warm and kind.

Adam smiled back. "I hope you will reach safety, soon. May you go with God."

The old herder walked lithely to the front of his flock and started toward the hills. He turned for a moment and waved his dark hand to Adam. "*Hasta la vista, mi amigo*." The words floated across the hot still air.

Adam smiled and waved back. "*Hasta la vista,* señor." He hoped they really would meet again.

11

THE DUST from the retreating goat herd rose languidly in the still air and hung there until it blended into the silver haze that was filling the brushland. Adam walked toward the mail station. His muffled steps in the thick dust made him suddenly aware of the stillness around him. Not a bird sang. Not a cricket chirped. It seemed to him as if everything was holding its breath. Sweat trickled down his cheeks from the heat that enveloped him like a blanket. He looked anxiously over his shoulder at the dark sky, ominous and forbidding in the north. *La vaca*, as Feliz had called it, was spreading upward until now it covered a quarter of the sky.

Adam padded faster toward the camp. He glanced back at Reba, who followed him, her tail down, her tongue hanging out. Each step she took seemed to be an effort. Adam patted her head. "I know how you feel, Reba, but just wait. It'll cool off directly."

Inside the mail station, Adam picked up the ax and gave the tent stakes several heavy blows to pound them in deeper. He tested the tent ropes to make sure they

170

would not slip off the stakes. He knew what a vicious and powerful wind a norther could be. With his knife, he cut the meat off the armadillo and threw the carcass to Reba. She dragged it about the camp, looking for a likely place to bury it. He put the armadillo meat into the skillet, fastened the lid on securely, and took it into the tent. He pulled back the rumpled covers on his cot, reached over for the sacks of supplies, and laid them along the cot pad. Placing the skillet on top, he pulled the covers over the supplies and tucked the quilts under the pad. There. That should keep the food from becoming gritty from the dust that the wind would blow into every nook and cranny.

With the empty bucket in his hand, he headed for the tank again. It would take several buckets of water to put the campfire out completely. Maybe he was foolish to waste time this way. If it were a wet norther, the rain would put the coals out in a few minutes. But if it weren't, a live coal blown into the brush could set the whole fence on fire, and maybe the whole brushland.

A hissing cloud of white steam rose into the air with each fan of water he threw on the fire. He watched the last red coal turn black and send its thin plume of steam upward. The acrid smell of the wet coals filled his nostrils, and he rubbed his nose against his damp sleeve. Suddenly the air around him seemed slightly cooler. He glanced up. The edge of the storm cloud was creeping across the sun, turning it blood red. For a few moments the sky became suffused with yellow and orange and deep gold; then the colors faded and the sun disappeared

171

altogether in the steely gray trap that seemed to be closing on the brushland.

Adam glanced at the hills to the north. They had disappeared completely into inky blackness. Before them hung a gray-green veil that seemed to undulate and billow like a lace curtain at an open window. A cool breeze blew across Adam's cheek, and he lifted his head to let it blow across his sweaty neck. The canvas tent flap began to snap back and forth. The chickens that had been dusting themselves near the fence opening rose and waddled toward the lee of the tent. The breeze swirled their bared feathers apart in places so that Adam could see their pink skin.

The wind was growing stronger and colder. Adam felt suddenly free of the oppressive heat, and he held his arms out to let the delicious coolness flow about his damp body. Reba seemed to notice the change too, and ran barking after a small branch of hog plum that had blown loose from the fence and rolled across the compound. All at once, Adam became aware of a roar that sounded like a railroad train in the distance. He glanced back at the storm. Little wisps of white clouds, like pieces of torn paper, were scudding across the blackness. It was growing darker, too.

A larger branch of hog plum toppled from the fence and skipped across the camp to wedge itself against the other side. Adam felt prickles about his ankles and looked down. The dust was blowing across his feet in a blur of yellow, like muddy water. His clothes flapped about him, and he began to shiver in the cold wind that was beginning to whistle through the brush fence. He could hear the rope on the tent stakes creak as the increasing gusts set the tent billowing like a sail. The roar was growing steadily louder.

Reba crept toward Adam, her tail between her legs, her ears streaming back from her head. Adam thought perhaps he should catch the chickens and put them in the tent. He started forward. A large branch of mesquite tumbled off of the fence and slid across in front of him. Unable to stop, Adam stumbled over it and fell heavily into the streaming dust. The powdered caliche filled his nose and burned like pepper. Before he could get to his feet, another thorny branch tore loose and blew across his back, tearing his shirt and leaving long scratches on his thin body. Adam looked up in alarm. Was his brush fence going to blow away completely?

It was as dark as evening now, and the roar was all around him. Near the fence opening, the top of the mesquite tree thrashed back and forth. A prickly pear cactus pad rolled by the opening like a wheel. Adam stood up and leaned into the wind, his head down, his hands shielding his eyes against the dust that filled the air now and stung his body. He found the chickens pressed against the brush fence, helpless to move in the violent wind. He picked them up, and with one tucked under either arm, managed to round the tent and carry them inside. He placed the Plymouth Rocks on the end of the cot, where they crouched down squawking with alarm at each loud snap of the tent canvas.

He ran outside and dragged the loose branches

173

back across the compound. He tried to push them into the fence, but as fast as he replaced the branches, the wind tore them loose again. Helplessly he watched his fence top blow away.

He felt the sudden cold splash of rain drops on his face. They came slanting in through the dust, thicker and thicker. The smell of wet earth swirled up from the ground, and he felt his shirt begin to stick to his shoulders where the big drops soaked into the cloth. Over the top of the fence, he could see the rain, pushed by the wind, slide like a thin gray drape across the brushland. It was raining harder now, and he ran for the tent. The caliche, wetted only on top, stuck to the soles of his feet.

In the gloom of the tent, Adam sat on the edge of his cot and listened to the creak of the straining tent ropes. The rain drumming on the canvas stopped as suddenly as it had started, but the wind continued to whistle and whine outside. Reba leaned against Adam's bare legs, licking her wet fur. He could feel her shivering, too, in the growing cold. Adam wished he had brought a coat to wear. But then, how could anybody know there would be a norther this early in the season? He did have his boots somewhere. Adam leaned over and peered under the cot. Yes, there they were. He dragged them out, knocked them together upside down, and checked them carefully inside. He brushed the dried caliche from the bottom of his feet and, with grunts and groans, pulled the boots on. They seemed much tighter than he remembered them, but at least they would keep his feet warm.

174

Adam glanced outside. Despite the brief rain, the dust still swirled across the brushland. Stifling gusts blew through the mail station, filling his eyes and nose with the powdered caliche. He could feel it in his mouth when he gritted his teeth. The sky had lightened to slate gray now, and the wind was chill and raw. There was no way of telling what time of day it was, nor when his father would be arriving. What should he do about dinner? With such a strong wind still blowing, it wasn't safe to build a fire. Would his father be satisfied with the cold armadillo meat?

It was too cold to stay outside the tent for very long at a time, so that Adam didn't see his father's wagon approaching. Not until he heard the jingle of the harnesses and the stamp of the horses' hoofs did he realize that his father had arrived. Adam ran out of the tent. He held his arms across his chest to keep from shivering. His father was climbing down from the wagon, his hat pulled low over his eyes, the collar of his big range coat turned up around his ears.

Adam's father reached under the wagon seat and pulled out a rolled-up bundle. He turned to Adam. "Come here, Son, put this on before you catch your death of cold." It was Adam's heavy jacket.

Quickly, Adam stuck his blue-cold arms into the padded sleeves and, with numb fingers, fumbled at the buttons. "*Gracias*. The wind has indeed made me cold."

Joe Vance looked at his son quizzically. "What are you talkin' Spanish for?"

Adam grinned sheepishly. "I'm sorry, Pa, I forgot."

175

Adam's father glanced down. "I see you had sense enough to put your boots on." He started for the camp-fire but stopped. Only the blackened coals lay on the bare caliche between the iron supports. The ashes had blown away. He turned toward Adam. "What happened to the fire? You fresh out of matches?"

"I put it out, Pa."

"You what!"

"I put it out. I was afraid it might blow into the brush fence and set it on fire."

Adam's father put his hands on his hips. "Didn't you have sense enough to cover it?"

"With what? Dirt would have blown away."

Joe Vance looked disgusted. "You could have scraped the coals together, turned a bucket over 'em, and put a big rock on top."

"Wouldn't the bucket smother the coals?"

"Not likely with this wind. There'd be enough air comin' in underneath to keep 'em alive."

Adam wished he had thought of that. He looked up at his father. "I got some meat in the tent, Pa. I covered it so the dust wouldn't get in." Adam hurried inside the tent and pulled the skillet from under the quilts. He drew out the plates and cups, too, and set them on top of the covered supplies.

Adam's father came into the tent and blew on his fingers. He looked at the lumpy bundle in the middle of the cot. "Now what in tarnation is that?"

"The food supplies, Pa. I covered them to keep the dust out."

"Well, at least *that* was smart thinkin'." Joe Vance lifted the skillet lid. "What's this?"

"Armadillo meat."

"Armadillo! When did you bag *that*?"

"I didn't. There was the Mexican goatherder came by. He got it with his sling last night. We shared our supper."

Adam's father picked gingerly at the meat with his fingers. "Never thought much of armadillo." He handed a cup to Adam. "Here, Son, fetch me some water."

Adam stepped quickly outside to the water barrel. The dipper had blown off into the fence. He picked it up and came back. When he lifted the lid, he saw that the surface of the water was dull with dust. He reached deep and brought the dipper out quickly. Dust particles eddied in the water. He tried again, but the next dipperful was no better. He poured it into the cup and took it to his father.

Joe Vance peered at the liquid. "This looks like tank water."

"I'm sorry, Pa. There's dust in the water barrel, too. If I had a prickly pear pad, though, I could clarify the water. Feliz showed me how."

"Who's Feliz?"

"He's the Mexican goatherder I told you about. He stayed all night with me."

"Where did he bed down his goats?"

"Over in the new clearin'."

Adam's father frowned. "You let him put dirty goats in there?"

177

"They weren't dirty, Pa."

"Well, Son, after you've finished cleanin' the goat droppin's out of there, you'll change your mind. And you'd better get it done pronto. Seth and I are fixin' to move you in there tomorrow." Joe walked to the tent opening and squinted across the murky brushland. "Seems like Seth should be here by now."

"Isn't that his wagon, Pa?" Adam pointed toward a blur of dust that was moving slowly toward the mail station. The wagon emerged slowly from the dust cloud, took solid shape, and lumbered noisily to a stop outside the brush opening.

Uncle Seth climbed from his wagon and swung his long arms back and forth across his chest. He was bundled in a range coat, but Adam could see that the cold wind had chilled his uncle, too.

Inside the tent, Uncle Seth took off his leather gloves and held his hands over his ears. "Whoo-ee! It's cold enough to freeze over Hades. You bring on this duster, Adam?"

Adam laughed. "No, Uncle Seth, but I knew it was comin'." He held out the armadillo meat to his uncle.

"Knew it was comin', eh?" Uncle Seth munched on the meat. "How's that?"

Adam told him of the forecasting rattlesnakes, the bright stars in the Milky Way, the coyotes howling after sunrise, the goats shaking themselves—all the signs Feliz had pointed out.

Uncle Seth turned to Adam's father. "We got ourselves a weather boy. And a mighty smart one, too. Ran into Sheriff Bradly last night and he told me all the

178

shenanigans Adam pulled to outsmart those jailbreakers when they came back here that second time. Listen to this, Joe. . . ."

At the mention of the jailbreakers coming back, Joe Vance looked sharply at his son. Adam ducked his head and hurried out of the tent to get his uncle a cup of water while the men talked. That squirmy feeling in his stomach was back again. Maybe he should have told his father about the outlaws' second visit, but it was too late now.

When he entered, Uncle Seth drank the water and pulled his gloves on. "Got to head back to Rio Verde directly. One of my horses threw a shoe." He pulled his hat low on his forehead and stepped out into the steady wind.

Adam's father followed him, and together they exchanged the mailbags. There wasn't time to water the horses at the tank. Instead, Adam brought them each a pailful from the precious water in the barrel.

Uncle Seth turned his wagon around and waved to Adam and his father. "With the wind at my tail, I'll be home before you will today, Joe." The wagon melted into the dusty brushland.

Adam's father turned to him. His face was stern. "Why did you lie to me, Adam?"

"What are you talking about, Pa?"

"You know what I'm talking about, Son!"

"No, honest!"

"Those outlaws that you said didn't come back here . . . when they *did*."

"I didn't say that, Pa."

"No?"

"I said they didn't come back while the posse was here! That's what I said! It's the truth!"

Adam could see the muscles working in and out on his father's jaws. Sharp blue eyes drilled into Adam like the cold wind that penetrated his jacket. His father's voice was low. "But only half the truth, Son, and half truths undercut a person's character same as a lie."

Adam hunched his shoulders. "I don't see how!"

Joe Vance reached out and gripped his son's arms. The vicelike hold of his father's fingers hurt Adam even through his jacket. His father's face was close to his. "A half truth undercuts like a gully washin' under the corner of a shed. Each time it rains, a little more dirt washes away until the shed falls into the hole. Half truths become less and less truths until they're no truths at all." Adam's father released him. "If there's one thing I don't want you to be, it's a lyin' son!"

Adam's throat swelled and his eyes stung. The squirming feeling in his stomach had turned into a pulsing ache. All the lonely terrifying moments of that night with Dugan and Slate surged back into his mind. His voice rose above the whistling wind. "You don't understand, Pa, you just don't understand! If I'd told you how much Dugan and Slate scared me that night, you wouldn't have let me stay at the mail station. You kept sayin' I wasn't big enough for the job . . . you wanted to get someone else. Well, I *proved* I was big enough. I *proved* it!"

Joe Vance's voice sounded taut as a wire. "You

only proved one thing, Adam: that I shouldn't have let you come out here by yourself in the first place! This is no job for a young 'un!"

Unreasoning rage filled Adam. "You don't *want* me to grow up! You want me to stay little so you can boss me around! Well, I've fooled *you*! I sure enough have! I've grown up anyway. I took care of those criminals all right—better than a grownup, maybe!"

Adam's father shook his head slowly. "That's no grownup talkin'; that's just a braggin' boy." He turned and started for the mail wagon.

A sudden gust of wind caught under the brim of his hat and lifted it from his head. Adam's father reached for the hat but missed. It sailed through the air, landed on the ground, and flopped over and over across the bare caliche. It lodged under a mesquite branch at the bottom of the brush fence. He strode across and bent down to pick his hat up.

Above the rushing wind, Adam heard his father cry out. Adam turned quickly. Joe Vance knelt by the brush fence, his face drained suddenly white. Fastened to his right hand was the ugly head of a big diamond-backed rattler.

12

ADAM stood staring at the snake, unable to move. His father reached over with his free hand, seized the scaly body that coiled about his arm, and wrenched the rattler loose. He stood up quickly, threw the snake to the ground, and stamped on the hissing head with his heavy boot. He turned toward Adam, his right wrist held tightly.

"Adam!" His father spoke hoarsely. "A chicken! Bring me a chicken, quick!"

The fear in his father's voice pierced the resentment in Adam, and his anger drained away quickly. He ran toward the tent.

"Hurry!"

Adam scooped up one of the hens near the edge of the cot and brought it outside.

"Now kill it, quick!"

Adam looked at his father in disbelief. "Kill it?"

"Yes, kill it . . . the ax . . . there by the tent."

"But Pa . . . we need . . ."

"I said *kill* it!" Joe Vance sucked in his breath, and

his eyes widened with pain.

Adam seized the ax, laid the squawking hen on the ground, and chopped its head off. Adam's father stood over him. Adam could see his father's knees were trembling.

"Cut its breast open." There was urgency in his father's tone. Adam followed his father's orders.

"Hand it to me."

Adam could see that his father's right hand was swelling rapidly. Red streaks ran out from the wound and up toward the wrist. Seizing the chicken, Joe Vance plunged his right hand into the cavity Adam had cut, and held the hen's body tightly around the wound.

He noticed the astonishment in Adam's face. "Draws the poison out," he murmured through lips tight with pain.

Adam rose to his feet. "We got to get you to Doc Anders, Pa." He could see that his father was shaking all over now. Adam's own knees were shaking, too. He ran into the tent, pulled the quilts off the supplies, and brought them out. He draped them across his father's shoulders.

Joe Vance started to walk toward the wagon. A blast of icy wind gusted across the mail station, and he staggered into the side of the tent. Adam seized his father's arm and guided him toward the fence opening. He helped his father pull his big frame onto the wagon seat, then jumped up beside him and tucked the quilts around his father's knees.

Joe Vance groaned and turned toward Adam. "The

183

other chicken. Fix the other chicken."

With a jump, Adam landed on the ground and ran for the tent. In a few moments he returned and handed the limp hen to his father. Adam faced away, shuddering, and wiped his bloody hands on his jeans. The Winchester! He mustn't forget that. What else would he need? Water, maybe? He grabbed the bucket, filled it from the water barrel, and threw the dipper into the pail. The water slopped over the edge and soaked his jacket sleeves when he slid the bucket under the wagon seat. He ran back for the Winchester and called Reba. With the gun stowed under the seat, Adam lifted Reba into the wagon bed. She stuck her head over the edge and peered questioningly at Adam.

Adam's father was leaning forward, holding his arm. There wasn't time to get anything else. Adam ran around to the other side of the wagon, climbed onto the seat, and with the reins held firmly in one hand, released the wagon brake and clucked to the horses. The wagon lurched forward, and Adam headed the horses into the wind.

The road to Ryansville, two deep ruts winding through the brush, was familiar to the horses, and Adam urged them into a trot. They threw their heads forward and snorted puffs of white steam into the bitter air. Their manes streamed back darkly, and for a moment, Adam watched the ripple of their powerful muscles under their shiny hides. He glanced about the brushland. Beside the road, the wagon-high thickets of mesquite and guajillo swayed stiffly back and forth in the

wind. Wrapped in swirling dust, they seemed to Adam like gray-shawled shoulders of ghosts rocking with laughter. Adam squinted ahead. There were no hills anywhere, only gray brushland and gray sky fastened together at the edges.

The wagon jolted over a rock, and Adam heard his father groan. He glanced at him. He had fallen forward and was leaning perilously over the front edge of the wagon. Adam pulled back on the reins. The horses snorted to a stop. He grabbed his father by the shoulders. "Watch out, Pa, let me help you back." But when he tugged at the broad shoulders, there was no response, and he realized that his father was unconscious.

Adam tried to reach across his father and push him back, but his father hung out of the wagon too far. Bracing himself directly behind the limp body, Adam lifted his father under the arms and strained backward. The inert form yielded slowly. Adam stopped to get his breath. It was too dangerous to prop his father up in the seat. He might fall forward again. Adam thought if he could lift the big man over the back of the seat into the wagon box, he could make a bed for him there with the quilts.

Tugging again, Adam managed to prop his father against the seat. He climbed onto the seat and dragged his father up and back, then clambered into the wagon bed, hooked his arms under his father's arms, and pulled with all his might. Inch by inch, he slid his father's unconscious form over the seat back. He had never realized how heavy his father was. He had to stop frequent-

186

ly to catch his breath and to quiet his quivering muscles.

A loud clump, and his father's boots hit the wagon bed. Adam nearly fell under the full weight of the huge form. He lowered his father to the wagon floor and knelt panting beside him. It took only a few minutes to spread a quilt, pull his father onto it, and tuck another quilt about him. Adam was careful to keep the wounded hand free. The chicken carcass still clung to the hand, and he could see that the edges of the chicken's breast had turned black with the poison.

Adam dragged the mailbag across the wagon and propped his father's head against it. His father groaned and opened his eyes. His lips were swollen and his face red and puffy. Despite the bitter cold, beads of sweat stood out on his temples. He whispered something, and Adam bent down to hear the words above the roar of the wind.

"Water!" The lips formed the word again.

Adam reached for the dipper in the water bucket. His hand shook, and he left a trail of spilled drops as he brought the liquid across the wagon bed. His father drank eagerly and, leaning back, looked about.

"Where am I?"

"In the wagon bed."

"How did I get here?"

"You fainted and nearly fell out of the wagon. I had to drag you back."

Joe Vance looked incredulously at Adam. "You lifted me over the wagon seat all by yourself?"

Adam nodded.

His father turned his head away and closed his eyes. Reba came over and laid her head on Adam's knee. He patted her, and she curled up on the quilt beside Adam's father. Adam stood up and climbed back into the wagon seat. He slapped the reins against the horses' backs, and the wagon rolled forward again.

The sky was growing darker. It was hard to tell whether evening was coming, or another storm squall. Adam had lost all sense of time since the blood-red sun had disappeared that morning. He wondered where Feliz was now. Beguiling Feliz and his capering goats. Had he reached the protection of the hills in time? Adam hoped so. Why had he liked Feliz so much? he wondered. Was it his stories? His vast knowledge of the chaparral? Perhaps. But there was something else. It was how he had looked at Adam. How he had talked to him. He had called him *mi amigo*, my friend, not *muchacho*, boy. Feliz had made him feel equal with him, and Feliz was a man. That was it! Feliz had made him feel like a man.

Adam glanced over his shoulder at the still form of his father in the wagon bed. Why couldn't his father think of him that way, too? Would he always be a *muchacho* to his father? What did a son have to do to show his father he was his equal?

The light was almost gone from the sky. In the gray gloom of the brushland, the swaying clumps of mesquite and coma looked to Adam like the restless backs of cattle before a thunderstorm. The first thin coyote wail, blown by the cold wind through the thorny chaparral, seemed to shred into a thousand whining voices. Adam, high on the wagon seat, hunched his shoulders forward and held his arms close against his body. His wet jacket sleeve had chilled his arm until it ached with cold. He wished he had mittens to wear. His hands were growing so numb he could hardly feel the reins. He could smell the pungent odor of damp harness leather. The horses were quickening their gait. They must know they were nearing home.

Above the wind, Adam heard his father retch and gasp loudly. Adam reined the horses to a stop and looked over his shoulder. He could hear his father still gasping for air. Was he dying? In alarm, Adam stumbled over the wagon seat and knelt beside his father. In the dim light, he could see his father's eyes were closed. His face shone ghostly white, and he breathed in short panting gasps.

"Pa! Pa!" Adam seized his father's shoulders.

Joe Vance opened his eyes briefly, then closed them again.

A chilling fear clutched at Adam. What ever would he do without his father? There was so much he had yet to learn. Suddenly, in the gloom of the wagon bed, as though looking into a mirror, Adam saw himself. He wasn't grown up at all! He wasn't an equal of his father's. He never would be.

Adam laid his head against his father's chest and heard him draw several long breaths. Then he felt his father's good hand tousle his hair. Adam looked up and peered closely into his father's face. The big man's eyes were open again. His voice was husky when he spoke. "I'm sorry, Adam."

"About what, Pa?"

"Lost my temper . . . had no call to."

"I did too, Pa. Reckon the wind riles a body up."

"You're a good son, Adam."

"I got a lot to learn. I'm not as grown up as I thought I was."

"That proves it."

"Proves what?"

"That you *are* growin' up."

"I don't get it, Pa."

"There's an old sayin'. 'The older a person grows, the more he realizes how little he knows.'"

Adam smiled in the darkness. "Reckon that's so."

Joe moved his swollen arm under the quilt. "We almost home?"

"Almost, Pa." Adam tucked the quilt under his father's chin. "We'll be there directly." He scrambled back into the wagon seat. "Hup!" he called sharply to the horses, and with a creak of leather, they lurched forward again.

The lights of Ryansville glowed as the wagon rounded the next turn. The ruts turned into a smooth road bed, and the tossing silhouettes of guajillo gave way to neat rows of bending fernlike chinaberry trees.

Adam drove the wagon through the deserted square and down a wind-tossed street to a white clapboard house with a gallery around it. A kerosene lamp was

190

glowing on the table near the window. Adam stopped by the front steps, jumped down, and ran to the door. "Juanita! Becky!" he called.

He heard steps hurrying through the house. A dark plump woman with a black shawl about her shoulders opened the door and flung her arms around Adam. "Oh, Adam!" she cried. Then she held him at arm's length and alarm filled her dark eyes. "What is wrong? Where is your papa?"

"In the wagon. A rattler bit him."

"*Santa Maria!*" Juanita crossed herself and hurried to the tailgate. She turned to the slender girl who had followed her out. "Go, Becky, fetch Doctor Anders. Here, take this." She pulled the shawl from her shoulders and handed it to Becky, who threw it over her head and ran off into the darkness.

Adam released the tailgate, and Reba licked his face while he swung the gate down. He gathered her into his arms and set her on the ground where she ran about jumping excitedly on everyone. Together Adam and Juanita struggled to move Joe to the edge of the wagon, pulled him down, and half-dragged, half-carried him into the house. In a few minutes Doc Anders came puffing up the steps, with Becky right behind him.

Joe lay on the bed with his swollen arm filling his coat sleeve. He had lost consciousness again. Adam stood beside Becky at the foot of the bed. He gripped the brass knob, his knuckles white.

Doc Anders peered over the tops of his glasses at Adam. His voice was crisp. "Becky, take that brother of yours out to the kitchen and get some warm vittles into him, or I'll have another patient on my hands. Juanita, you stay here and help me."

Adam sat at the kitchen table staring at the red-checked cloth. The bowl of chili Becky had heated for him stood uneaten. Dr. Anders had been with his father several hours now. When would he come out? Adam put his head down on his arms. He felt suddenly old and he didn't want to be. What a lot had happened in the last six days in the mail station! Funny how scared he had been that first night. He really *was* a boy then! What had changed him? he wondered. The coyotes? The rattlesnakes? Slate and Dugan? His father's accident?

The bedroom door opened, and Dr. Anders shuffled into the kitchen. Adam raised his tired eyes to the doctor's face. "Will he be all right?"

Doc Anders pulled a chair over and sat facing Adam. The gold rims on the doctor's glasses glinted in the lamp light as he shook his head. "Lots of poison in that arm . . . must have been a daddy of a rattler." He reached over and patted Adam's hand. "But I wouldn't fret about him, Adam. You Vance men are mighty tough *hombres*. You could lasso a whole den of rattlers and train them to string fencewire in six weeks."

Relief coursed through Adam, warming every bone. He looked into Doc Anders' smiling face and grinned slowly. "I reckon we could do *that* in six days."

192

Date Due
